"Are you dancin'?" Anni asked

When Max didn't answer at once, she added, "Don't you know how it goes? You're supposed to say 'Are you askin'?'"

"I have heard it." He smiled down at her and his skin looked even darker against his white jacket and shirt. "Are you askin'?"

"Yes," she said. "Oh, yes." She went into his arms—and after that first halting step, it was everything she'd known it would be. In the circle of his arms, she was lost. Her cheek rested on his shoulder. She thought his lips brushed her hair and she felt her heart stop with delight. She looked up at him smiling, and said, "You dance well."

"I don't," he said. "But you lie beautifully. And you dance beautifully, too."

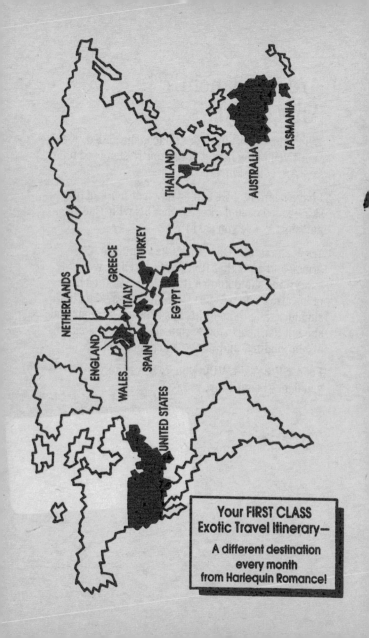

NETHERLANDS
THAILAND
TURKEY
GREECE
ITALY
EGYPT
AUSTRALIA
TASMANIA
ENGLAND
WALES
SPAIN
UNITED STATES

Your FIRST CLASS
Exotic Travel Itinerary—

A different destination
every month
from Harlequin Romance!

THE JEWELS OF HELEN

Jane Donnelly

Harlequin Books

TORONTO • NEW YORK • LONDON
AMSTERDAM • PARIS • SYDNEY • HAMBURG
STOCKHOLM • ATHENS • TOKYO • MILAN

Original hardcover edition published in 1990
by Mills & Boon Limited

ISBN 0-373-03128-9

Harlequin Romance first edition June 1991

THE JEWELS OF HELEN

CHAPTER ONE

When the knock came on the door Anni Bradford thought it was surely too soon for Max Torba to have driven from London to Oxford. It seemed no time at all since he had said, 'I'll be right with you,' and hung up before she could stammer,

'I don't want you with me, I don't want to see you.'

Now Anni opened the door slowly and stared at the man whose powerful shoulders seemed to fill the doorway, while his head nearly touched the beam across the top. Max Torba had thick black curling hair, and his complexion was more tanned than she remembered. The forehead lines and the lines cutting from nose to mouth were deeper, but the strong mouth with the sensually curved upper lip was the same. She had not looked closely at him in eight years although he was regularly on television, but she thought she would still recognise him even after fifty years.

In appearance she had not changed that much herself. She was still tall and slender. High cheek-bones and a good bone-structure meant that she was almost beautiful. Her mid-brown hair had been long then. Now it was shorter, pushed or worn behind her ears, and the sun of this hot summer had streaked it with blonde strands. But her eyes, which were her best feature, an almost luminous grey, looked haunted and her face was smudged where she had rubbed grimy fingers across it.

She couldn't speak. The man looked down at her for a moment and then beyond her. 'My lord,' he said, and she stepped aside to let him pass. He walked into the middle of the room, taking it in in a quick glance.

'It was Roger's flat, wasn't it?' she said.

At the windows a feathering of dust edged the folds of the drawn-back curtains and dust lay on the leather armchairs, the dark red Indian carpet, the bookshelves, like a fine grey veil. Ever since she had managed to turn the key in the lock and walk in here a chill like death had been creeping through her, although the air was warm and musty.

'Yes,' he said. 'What happened? Or what didn't happen? Why this?'

'Because my father wanted it to stay this way, I suppose. An agency was dealing with everything. They were told it was store-rooms. The rest of the house is bedsits, students mostly.'

'And you had no idea?'

'I didn't even know he owned the house until last week.' It was nearly a year since her father had died, of a massive coronary in his sleep, and she explained, 'He didn't leave a will.'

Torba would be thinking that an intelligent man should have had his affairs in better order even if there was only one living relative. And Anni could hardly say, 'I'm lucky he didn't. If he had done he would not have named me in it.'

Discovering that the house was a four-storey Georgian in a Regency square had been a pleasant surprise, but when she had opened this door and seen the painting that had been in Roger's room at home for a while, and smelt the mustiness and touched the grime, she had known that this apartment was how her brother must have left it when he went off to Austria with Max Torba on that skiing holiday from which he had never returned.

She said, 'You needn't have come all this way. I shouldn't have rung you.'

'No trouble.' It would be no distance to someone who was usually travelling the world, and when she'd phoned him she had not been thinking clearly at all. She had gone round the rooms, opening cupboards and drawers, looking for goodness knew what, some word from Roger maybe, and among some snaps in a bureau was one of Roger in a group of young men and women. One of the men was Max Torba; she didn't recognise anyone else, and she had gone downstairs to the coin-box telephone and dialled his number.

When her father died Torba had been among those who had sent her a letter of condolence, and she could not imagine why his London phone number had stuck in her head because she had never intended to get in touch with him. When she heard the deep voice that always made her turn off the radio or the TV, her own voice sounded strangely high-pitched. 'This is Annabel Bradford, Gerald Bradford's daughter. I've just found an old photograph with Roger on it, and you and some others. If I sent it on to you, would you try to remember who they were for me? I'd like to get in touch with them.'

He said, 'Of course,' and then, 'Is anything the matter?'

'I'm at fourteen Qualtrough Gardens, Oxford. I'd never been here until today and I've just opened the door of an apartment to find it's just how Roger left it all those years ago. There are even newspapers.'

'You're not alone there?'

'Yes.'

'I'll be right with you.' He hung up and she knew that she should phone again and stop him, but now she couldn't even remember his number. Digits danced in her brain, forming all sorts of combinations; her head was aching and her hands were shaking. Of course she wanted to stop him coming, but how could she?

She was still shaking now while she was fighting for control. She babbled, 'Is it how you remember it? I knew he had digs here as an undergraduate but I never came down; there was quite an age gap between us. You used to come here, did you?'

'We all did.' They had been at college together. Roger had got a creditable second and Max Torba had finished with a double first. But Roger had been talented too, and the future had looked promising for him. Anni picked up the photograph.

'Roger's on this. And you. Do you recognise anyone else?' Suddenly she wanted to get in touch with someone who would talk about her brother. It was seeing all his things, his books, even clothes in the bedroom cupboard, that made her loss seem piercingly fresh in this room for all its air of decay.

Not Max Torba though. She didn't want him close to her in any way and as he reached for the snapshot, looming over her, she let go of it so quickly that it fluttered to the floor. He stooped to pick it up and she mumbled, 'I need a coffee, I wonder——'

There was half a jar of solidified instant in the kitchen cupboard. She reached it down, and tried to turn on a tap, which seemed to have solidified too. Behind her Max Torba said, 'I think you should get out of here.'

She must be filthy, handling things, pushing her hair back, rubbing the back of her hand over her eyes. 'I'm all right,' she said, her fingers stiff around the tap that had not been turned for eight years, with a jar of coffee as hard as a rock, and a wave of nausea swept over her so that she sagged and gagged, clutching the edge of the sink.

She must not faint, she never fainted. But the room was tilting and she was sliding, and she didn't know when he caught her although she came round as he was carrying her towards the sofa. Her faced was pressed against his shoulder and she jerked back her head, away from him, gasping. 'Put me down.'

'Hold it.' He held her upright with one arm, slipping off his jacket and dropping it over the dusty cushions. 'Now sit down.'

'What made me *do* that?' She had to sit for a

moment, burying her face in her own hands, beads of cold perspiration breaking out on her forehead.

'The air's poisonous. Can you walk?' She stood up, and he was right, it was fetid in here. 'Come on, we'll find somewhere you can clean up, and we'll have a meal.'

'I'm going home.'

She was not sitting through a meal with him, but when he said, 'Later,' she thought she would wait until she got outside before she stood up to him.

Locking the door after them, she found the key was even harder to turn this time, or her grip was weaker. When he said, 'Let me,' she had to drop her hand or he would have put his fingers over hers and she would have started shivering again.

Of course he turned the key and, she thought sourly, He could probably put his shoulder to the door and shove it in, he's built like an all-in wrestler. She held out her hand for him to drop in the ring of keys so that he didn't have to touch her, and as they started to walk downstairs a door opened below and a girl in jeans came out looking up towards them asking, 'Is the top floor let, then?'

'Yes,' said Anni. Let to a ghost for the past eight years.

The girl was looking at Max and she sounded breathless, asking, 'You are Max Torba, aren't you?'

She must have let him in, Anni reckoned, and

since then she had waited, door ajar, to hear him coming down again. 'That's right,' he said.

She was fluttering her eyelashes behind big round spectacles. 'I just had to tell you, I think your stuff's amazing, fantastic.'

'Thank you.'

'Gosh, you're even taller in real life, aren't you?' The girl giggled, and then, still swooning over Max, she gave Anni a puzzled sidewards glance and Anni said, 'I'm nobody.' She could have been Roger Bradford's sister. He could have been as big a name as this man given a few more years, and outside the house she said drily, 'I suppose you're always being told you're amazing.'

'Not always as a compliment.'

He smiled, and she thought, Your smile hasn't changed. It was always slow and relaxed, the kind of smile that made other people smile back, but it was still the smile on the face of the tiger. She said, 'I want to go home,' and knew how childish she was sounding and how she must look with her grubby face. If the girl with the spectacles had not been so dazzled by the sight of the famous Max Torba she would have wondered why the girl with him needed a wash.

A wash and a cup of coffee. Before Anni got behind the wheel of a car she really did need a cup of coffee.

'What did you have for breakfast?' Max Torba was asking, and she opened her mouth to say, 'I did have breakfast,' but he was looking hard at her and she hadn't the strength for even a small lie.

She said, 'A cup of tea, but I don't want anything to eat.'

She wished he would leave her so that she could creep away somewhere by herself, but he was not going to do that. When he took her arm she went with him because she couldn't face an argument—whoever won an argument against him anyway? And she needed all her control not to make a spectacle of herself shrieking, 'Don't *touch* me.'

Quite soon he said, 'This will do,' and they turned beneath a pink awning into a pink-walled restaurant.

'See you,' she said mechanically and headed for the Ladies'. It was empty, and pretty in pastel shades. She washed her hands and got rid of some of the grime, although she had to rub hard to remove the rest which was sticky and tacky. She cleaned the smears off her face with a tissue but she wouldn't feel clean until she had been under a hot shower—and this was all on the surface.

The pain that had been waiting for her in that room was inside her now, and as if that weren't enough she had conjured up the man who embodied the blackest memories. She had believed she would have done anything to avoid coming up against him and yet in a state of shock she had dialled his number. Now he was waiting for her and she had to sit opposite him and talk to him.

She looked longingly at the little window and wished this were a TV movie where folk were always going to a wash-room and escaping through little windows. But her only way out was through the door and she must be sensible. She could try pretending that Max Torba was just an ordinary man and that their paths had never crossed before. Except that there was nothing ordinary about him.

So, he was a celebrity she was interviewing. She had done plenty of that, talking and listening her way through shared lunches. She ran a comb through her hair, found a lipstick in her purse and touched her lips with it, then her cheeks because she was still pale enough to look haggard.

She rubbed her cheeks into what looked like a natural glow, breathed deeply and slowly, then straightened up and walked out into the restaurant.

He was watching for her, at a table by the window. She could feel herself churning with resentment under a façade of calm. She had to force herself to walk towards him and, when she reached him and he stood up drawing out a chair for her, there was a moment when she looked at that chair and nearly ran.

Then she sat down. This had to be got through and he could hardly be enjoying it either. He might feel a little sympathy for Roger's sister— that locked-up apartment had been a shocker. But he didn't like her either. Eight years ago he had told her what he thought about her and that was another memory she had tried to forget.

Now she had to be civilised and play it cool and she shook her head over the menu. 'I can't drink,

I'm driving, and I'm not really hungry. Anything will do.'

The waiter looked pained, brightening as Max Torba ordered, wasting no time on her. Food was going to be put in front of her whether she ate it or not. She turned in her chair, pretending to be interested in some water-colour country scenes hanging on the walls because she did not want to sit looking at him. He made her nervous. He was very still, but she was acutely aware of him even when she almost had her back to him.

When a cold soup was set in front of her she swallowed a little—chilled cucumber, minted. It was a hot day, and the soup was pleasant. She was a long way from hungry but it made sense to eat something before she drove home. Although unless someone had taken charge she would have gulped a coffee and set off light-headed jangling with nerves. And possibly had an accident because it was that kind of day.

As the salmon steaks came she looked across at him and wondered if he would have broken the silence or simply fed her and sent her on her way.

She said, 'You were right, I am steadying down.'

'Good,' he said, and took the photograph out of his pocket. 'I haven't kept in touch with all of them, but I'm sure these would like to hear from Roger's sister.'

He tore a page out of a pocket book, and wrote names, phone numbers, addresses, and she said, 'You can remember, just like that? I sometimes find it hard to remember my own number.'

He smiled and she thought, He believes me, he always thought I was stupid. She bit her lip because she had asked for that, looking down at the photograph taken nearly ten years ago. Roger would never grow old, and the young man who had been Max Torba hadn't changed that much, towering over them all. He was a giant then, with the same strong mouth and jawline and dark eyes under darker brows.

In the snapshot he was casually dressed, in a check open-necked shirt. Now he was wearing a superbly cut suit and a plain dark tie that looked like silk over a white shirt that certainly was. But the powerful shoulders inside the jacket were the same, hard muscled as an athlete, and the hands. She remembered the long, strong fingers, the square thumbnails, although that was odd because she couldn't remember ever really looking at his hands before.

It was one of those early Instamatic snaps, turning sepia although it had been lying in the darkness of a desk drawer. 'I wish it were a better one of Roger,' she said wistfully. His handsome young face was fading while Max Torba's almost brutal life force seemed to grow stronger all the time. How unfair it was. She couldn't hold down a sigh and she said, in some sort of explanation, 'But I don't need a photograph to remember him, I'll always remember how brave he was. He warned the rest of you, didn't he? He saved you all.'

Max Torba said quietly, 'Yes. He did.'

It had comforted her father and made him even

more proud of his son. After the accident Max
Torba had come straight from the airport to the
house where Gerald Bradford was mourning the
only living soul he had loved, and told them how
Roger had seen the danger and shouted a warning. His companions had gone for their lives, but
the white wave had drowned Roger and the waste
of his death appalled Anni still. She had always
thought that hesitation had cut off her brother's
escape, and as Max Torba became famous over
the years she had begrudged his arrogant strength
and his easy success because Roger had been just
as brilliant. Max Torba was alive because Rog was
dead and she could never forgive him.

For that, and other reasons, he had been the
last man in the world she wanted to meet again,
but now she was having lunch with him and he
was asking, 'What are you doing these days?'

After eight years anyone would ask that; it
didn't mean he wanted to know. She didn't need
to ask because he was Max Torba and she was not
giving him a chance to patronise her. She must
look washed-out, but her slick summer suit carried
a good designer label and she said brightly, 'I'm
doing very nicely, thank you. I'm a journalist. I
write for a women's mag, and I have fun and I get
around, and I have a darling little house with a
thumping great mortgage. My father sold the old
house and went abroad after——' she took a sip
of water '——after Rog died. You knew that?'

He nodded and she mused, 'Now I've got this
house he kept on. It brought in an income, I
suppose. And Roger's apartment that he locked

up and left. If I leave it as well perhaps I can pretend Rog is still there. Perhaps that was what my father did.'

She was talking to herself rather than to him. The rooms must be opened, and she knew what lay ahead of her when all Roger's personal belongings were brought out. It would be a terrible ordeal and she decided, 'I shall take a holiday first. To one of the Greek islands perhaps. Somewhere like that.'

She had time off owing, and then she could come back refreshed and stronger. She was fit and she was strong, but she was still in shock and she couldn't face it yet.

'How about Turkey?'

'What?' She had been thinking aloud, she wasn't asking for suggestions.

'I've a house in Nidus a few miles from Idessa. Down in the bay there's marine archaeology. Every summer a team arrives, exploring the remains of a city under the sea and staying in the villa. They've been doing it for years. You might get some copy out of that for your magazine.'

He pointed to a young man with a wide grin on the photograph. 'Jimmy Stapleton is there, he knew Roger. Anyhow, it's an invitation you might care to consider. The house is open. I'll be joining them myself shortly.'

She said, 'Thank you,' and was surprised to find that she had eaten most of her meal. 'I must go now. You've been very kind, I'm sure your time's valuable.'

He raised an eyebrow. 'Whose time isn't?' He

stood up as she did, settled the bill and was with her on the pavement while she was still trying to recall the way they had come. It wasn't far but she must have stumbled along like a sleep-walker.

'Where's your car?' he asked.

'In a car park.' She had had a ten-minute walk to Qualtrough Gardens. 'Where's yours?'

'Just outside the house.' Cars had been parked solidly round the square. He must have driven up just as one pulled out; he was the sort who would always find a parking space.

'I'll say goodbye, then,' she said.

'You're all right to drive?'

'Of course.'

She held out her hands and they were steady, and a couple passing did a double-take and a man said, 'You are Max Torba, aren't you? Saw you on the box last week.'

Anni got away, walking fast round the corner into a street of shops, taking the first turn, scurrying and hiding so that even if he had followed her almost immediately he would not have caught up with her.

Not that he would have followed—she had said goodbye—and after a while she went quietly to the car park and got into her car. It had been shock on shock. Roger's apartment and then Max Torba, and she would be hard put to it to say which had upset her more.

Some time she would have to deal with the apartment but with any luck at all she would not have to see the man again.

He had been sorry for her because she was the

sister of his old friend and she had just had a traumatic experience. But he had always despised her and on one thing she was absolutely determined. Wild horses would not drag her anywhere near that villa of his in Turkey.

CHAPTER TWO

THE heat was fierce as Anni waited for the *dolmus* in Idessa.

She was here as a journalist, there was nothing personal in it at all. Nothing at all to do with Max Torba. She had mentioned the city under the sea in the office and she was here to write about that. While she was taking a break she had decided that she might as well make it a working holiday.

The bus that came rattling along was almost full but she got aboard, where a smiling young man took her fare and poured a few drops of lemon cologne into her sticky palms, and she thanked him and found a seat next to a woman with a baby and a goat.

The *dolmus* stopped wherever it was hailed, some getting off as more passengers, animals, and chickens piled in. The scenery was breathtaking, mountainous hills rising on one side, and sometimes on the other a heart-stopping drop down to rocks and the ocean as they hugged the coastal road.

She had asked for Nidus when she paid her fare and half a dozen passengers were signalling her and calling. The woman with the baby poked her in the ribs to emphasise that she had arrived and she scrambled to her feet and jostled her way out.

This was hardly a village at all. A few dusty-looking houses faced the road. One man was getting on the bus and as Anni got off into the blazing sunshine she asked him, 'Max Torba's house?' He pointed for her, indicating white walls high up in the hills, and grinned toothlessly.

Down in the cove she could see where tents were pitched. There were boats out there and canoes drawn up on the shingle. One of the boats in deeper water might be anchored over the sunken city, and if she took the track leading down she could introduce herself to the team. If they were diving right now. Or she could go up to the villa, where Max Torba might be staying.

There was another track in that direction and after a moment's hesitation she began to climb.

Even if she reached the villa she might not knock on the door today. The message she had left on his answering machine in London had been that she would be in the area of the villa and that she would call, and for days now she had been telling herself that she could meet Max Torba again without the old bitterness. The accident had been a long time ago, and last week when he had come to her rescue in Roger's apartment had been a kindly gesture. She was grateful for that, although she had disliked him too long to ever find herself actually liking him. Anyhow, he might not even be in the villa. But, having come this far, she might as well have a look at his house.

The track was rough and rock-hard, winding but still a steep incline, and she made slow progress. It would have taken a mountain goat to nip

up here. When she stopped to draw breath she
could see women working in the fields below and
marvelled at their stamina. The sun was so hot
that she could feel it like a prickly rash on her
skin, and the hum of buzzing, stinging things
filled the air. But so did the scent of wild thyme
and it was magificent countryside.

She had passed a few houses on the lower
slopes but the house the man had pointed out was
surely at the end of the track, and that figured—
trust Max Torba to put himself at the top. Her legs
and back were aching after an hour's hard climbing when she finally stumbled up to the high
white wall.

She leaned against it, then jumped away
because it was burning hot and if she didn't get a
drink soon she could be expiring from dehy-
dration. She must have sweated gallons she was
so thirsty, and in a sudden burst of energy she
broke into a jog, running beside the wall, looking
for a way in.

The gates were open. Big gates in black scrolled
ironwork picked out in gold. But she hardly gave
them a glance because beyond the gate was a
shadowy courtyard with an orange tree growing,
and palms, and a magnolia.

The white villa stood in beautiful grounds, and
Anni walked through the gates enchanted by the
unexpectedness of it all. It was like stumbling on
paradise and there would probably be a fountain;
she thought she could hear running water.

Walking round the house she passed borders
and beds of geraniums, roses and lilies, and a

glorious climbing honeysuckle. It was pure magic. She breathed in the sweet, intoxicating scent of the honeysuckle, pulling off the little brimmed hat that was sticking to her forehead, shaking her hair free, and saw Max Torba standing at an upstairs window.

For a moment she couldn't move. She just stood there staring up. Even when he moved away she was still frozen, and then she shook herself with a little nervous jerk of the shoulders.

He had seen her and he was coming, and the reason her heart was racing was because she had just climbed up the mountain. She sauntered slowly towards a door but when he walked out it hit her again—the impact of a larger than life personality and physique combined with the resentment she couldn't help. It was as though he grabbed her by the shoulders, and her little social smile stiffened on her lips.

Fewer clothes didn't help either. He was wearing an open shirt, sleeves rolled up, trousers and sandals, and every inch of him looked macho male. 'So you did look us up,' he said.

'You got my message?'

'No.'

That wasn't her fault. She said, 'I rang your London number and spoke to your answering machine. Don't tell me something of yours doesn't work.'

'There's no phone up here and the mail is erratic. The messages get through eventually. I presume you didn't sound too urgent.'

So this fantastic place was a retreat where he

could get away from the pressures of life. You've got it all, she thought wryly. Nothing can ever have gone wrong for you. She said, 'You did suggest I could get a story out of the city under the sea. That's why I'm here, because my editor agreed with you. I'm staying in Idessa.'

'Why? Do you have friends there?'

'I didn't want to presume on your hospitality.'

He grinned slowly. His eyes were heavy-lidded in the bright light but she was obviously amusing him. 'You don't write as you talk, to you? It's a long time since I heard that cliché. How did you get up here?'

'I walked.'

'You look as if you did.' Of course she did. She was grubby, her cotton shift dress was sticking to her. She always seemed to be filthy when she met him. 'Where *are* you staying?' he asked her.

'A little hotel.'

'Of course you must stay here, there's plenty of room.'

She would enjoy resting in the garden for a while and she desperately needed a drink, but she could not imagine sleeping peacefully in one of Max Torba's beds and she hesitated, trying to come up with a reasonable excuse.

'It isn't always this quiet,' he said. 'Most of the time even you would find the company entertaining.' As if she needed lively folk around or she would be bored out of her empty mind. 'We're going into Idessa this afternoon. We'll collect your bags.'

THE JEWELS OF HELEN

No, he would not. But her throat felt sand-papered and she croaked, 'Could I have a drink, please?'

'Of course.'

Inside the villa the floor was marble mosaic in blues and jade. Sea colours, she thought, following him. She had taken off her sunglasses but the sudden change from blazing sunlight to shadowy cool meant that she had to blink to see clearly as she sank into the soft-cushioned seat.

She watched him go out of the room and as soon as she was alone she felt her muscles loosening and knew how tense she had been. When she met him again she should have been elegant and confident. Instead, with no one to blame but herself, she had arrived like someone on the run. A bite on her leg set up a flare of irritation and she resisted a temptation to scratch, although it was hotting up and adding to her discomfort.

When he handed her a glass he said, 'Fruit juice, you look punch-drunk enough,' and she gulped greedily. 'Sezer will show you a room.'

'I don't want——' She couldn't help sounding sullen and ungracious. She wanted to wash but she did not want to be allocated a room, and suddenly he grinned.

'Not exactly your scene, is it? You should have hired a mule or hitched a lift in the Range Rover.'

They wouldn't all be trekking up the mountain-side, of course he'd have transport. 'Could I do that?' she asked. 'Get a lift out?'

'Sure.'

'Book me a seat, will you?'

'At your service.' His tone was ironic. She was making a weak joke but he never had thought much of her sense of humour, and she wanted to say, 'You think you know it all, don't you? You thought you did then and you think you do now, but you know *nothing*.'

'I'll see you later,' he said as a woman came into the room.

Anni needed to freshen up and she needed a lift back so she muttered a grudging, 'Thank you.'

The woman wore a long, full grey skirt and a pink embroidered blouse. She had white hair and a merry brown wrinkled face. She beckoned and kept looking back and smiling as she went ahead up a wide flight of stairs to a gallery and along a corridor. She opened a door on a bathroom that looked a great improvement on the hotel's, and then another on a bedroom. At the bedroom door she stood aside until Anni stepped in, then she smiled again and went, closing the door.

The big double bed with white cotton pillows and sheets was tempting. After Anni had washed she might rest in here. If she went downstairs again Max Torba might be around. He could even feel that as she was a guest he should be paying her some sort of attention and, in spite of all her resolutions, there would always be something about him that got right under her skin.

Anyhow, who was she fooling? He wouldn't be playing the host to her and she wouldn't be staying here, although it was a lovely house and the gardens were magic.

She went to the window and raised the blind,

looking down on the gardens, and she could hear the faint clatter of typewriter keys. This room had to be on the same floor and quite near the window where she had seen him, so he had gone back to work, and she wondered what it was all about. She couldn't see him discussing much with her. He thought she was a featherbrain and she was stupid to let that bother her.

In the bathroom it was bliss to feel the grime and the stickiness floating away. She even found an after-bite lotion in a cabinet and dabbed the two red rising spots on her leg. Then she went back into the bedroom and stretched out on the bed.

The typing had stopped. She strained to listen and there was no sound at all. Maybe he was getting writers' block, but if he was it wasn't because of her. She didn't disturb him as much as a mosquito settling on his hand, and the mosquito hadn't been born that could get under his skin.

She wondered what could. Scratch Max Torba and you would strike granite, but the bed was soft and she let herself relax for a while.

She didn't think she slept but she must have done because at first when she opened her eyes she didn't know where she was. Then she remembered and got off the bed and went to the door. Walking along the corridor, she heard voices and, reaching the gallery, she could see Max Torba down there with a woman and three men.

As she started to go down the staircase he looked up and said, 'Good lord,' as if he had completely forgotten her. It was a long time since

she had been a non-person. It stirred up the bitter
memories but she smiled, putting out all the force
of her personality as he told them, 'This is
Annabel, Roger Bradford's sister.' Mentioning
Roger was for the benefit of the long, lean man
who advanced on her beaming and offering a
welcoming hand.

'Rog was a sweet feller, a very good friend.'

He had an American accent and Anni said, 'To
me too. You must be Jimmy Stapleton.'

'Yes, I am.' He seemed surprised. He must have
thought Roger had spoken of him, but he hadn't.
Max had told her he would be here.

'Jenny, Jimmy's wife.' Max Torba went on with
the introductions. 'Philippe Renaud, Henry
Whittaker.'

Anni shook hands and smiled. Max Torba
brought out the worst in her; she couldn't have
flirted or fooled with him to save her life, but she
liked the looks of the others and she wanted them
to like her.

The woman was a small, pretty blonde, her skin
tanned golden. Henry was sandy-haired and
freckled and Philippe was a dark-haired French-
man, dapper even in shorts and T-shirt.

Anni said gaily, 'Not Annabel, Anni. A, double
N, I and no E.' She grinned as she spelled it out.
'Well, Annabel is a bit of a mouthful; I thought
Anni was shorter and snappier. And I am a
journalist. Knock off the E and it could even get
noticed in print.'

She was laughing at herself and she made them
all laugh, but she felt that Max Torba was thinking

it was the affectation of a boring young woman. She didn't look at him. She looked at the others and said, 'Now, you'll be the diving team. I can't wait to hear about the excavations.'

'I'm afraid you'll have to wait,' Max Torba drawled. 'We're leaving now for Idessa. If you come along you can collect your luggage.'

As he had forgotten she was upstairs, that meant he would have gone without asking her if she wanted to stay here. As it happened this friendly bunch were beginning to change her mind and she explained to them, 'I booked into a little hotel last night. I could stay on there, I don't want to get in the way here.'

Henry declared gallantly that she could never be a nuisance and Jenny said that she would like another girl around.

'We shall all get on like the house on fire,' said Philippe, who prided himself on his grasp of the English language.

Anni agreed gaily, 'I'm sure we will and I'd love to stay; thank you for letting me.'

Max Torba said nothing. He was not going back on his invitation but his expression was quizzical, as if he was beginning to wonder if Anni might not turn out to be a problem.

The Range Rover was waiting outside, with Max in the driving seat and Henry beside him, as Jimmy and Jenny and Philippe helped Anni clamber aboard.

On the way Jimmy explained that Jen was a geologist and he was an archaeologist, both lecturers from the same Mid-Western university. Philippe was a marine photographer and Henry, who hailed from Yorkshire, was a deep-sea diver with an oil company. They had been coming here every summer for the last five years, staying at Max Torba's villa and joining a Turkish colleague to work on a long-term excavation of the city under the sea.

'We have not seen you here before,' said Philippe.

'I got my first invitation last week,' said Anni. If they hadn't known that it looked as if Max had not even bothered to mention her. The radio was tuned to a Turkish station and it was a noisy drive over a bumpy road. Max and Henry were talking so it was unlikely Max would overhear her telling them, 'He was quite surprised when I turned up. And he'd clean forgotten me again until I walked down the staircase.'

Jenny excused that, 'He had only just joined us himself. Of course he would have told us you were here and called you down before we left.'

Anni doubted it but she smiled and asked where they were heading. A newly built fishing boat was being launched that afternoon, they told her. The family were old friends of Max and they were off to join in the celebration. Nothing spectacular, just a friendly and festive send-off.

All the way they joked and chatted, finding interests in common, swapping stories. Jimmy had once been close to Roger, and she wanted him, his wife and his friends to accept her. She felt in a holiday mood in their cheerful company, and when they drew up on the waterfront the shining new boat had pride of place in the bay.

They were greeted on all sides—everyone seemed to be joining in the party and huge dishes of sweet cakes were being handed around. Finally, to cheers and raised glasses, the engines began to chug and the little boat set off under a cloudless sky.

It was fun. Anni was enjoying herself. She clinked a glass with Philippe and Max said, 'Go easy on that stuff.'

She was going easy. She knew what *raki* could to do you. She was laughing because she was happy, not because she was high, and she drained her glass defiantly and might even have taken another if Jenny hadn't said, 'That's about it. Shall we go and fetch your bags?'

As Anni walked with Jenny and Jimmy towards the small hotel and her luggage, a young man waved from across the road and she waved back.

'Who's that?' Jenny asked and Anni laughed.

'Gorgeous, isn't he?'

He was fair-haired and good-looking and last night, while she drank Turkish coffee at a small table in front of the hotel, Anni had chatted with him. They had exchanged names and wondered if they had met before, because he said he was an actor and in her job she often mixed in show-business circles. 'This is where I booked in,' she said. 'The bed wasn't bad but the bathroom was a shocker.'

She settled her bill and collected her cases and Jimmy took the larger one while she carried the other back to the car. Then she wandered around the old town with Jenny until it was time to meet

up with the rest again for an evening meal in a
courtyard that opened on to the waterfront.

The sun-bleached walls were covered with
purple bougainvillaea. It was all very pleasant and
Anni was able to relax because Max was not
sharing their table. He and Philippe were sitting
with the owner of the restaurant, and what looked
like several male members of the family. Unless
she turned she didn't have to see him at all.

As they dug into overloaded plates of food she
took the photograph out of an envelope in her
handbag and put it down in front of Jimmy.
'Recognise anyone?' she asked.

He leaned to look, then grabbed it up. 'Do I
not? Those were the days.' Jenny put a chin on
his shoulder to see and he said, 'Before your time,
hon. That's me. And Max. And Roger. This was
taken in a flat Roger had in Oxford.' He said it so
casually that she knew Max had not told him that
no one had opened that door in eight years.

He had been smiling but then he looked grave.
'This was just before we went skiing together.' He
sighed. 'Terrible. He was a great guy, your
brother.'

He reached across to give Anni's arm a quick
comforting squeeze. She hadn't known Jimmy
was in the party, but she was glad that Roger's
warning had helped to save Jimmy for Jenny; they
were a smashing pair.

'Where did this come from?' Jimmy asked and
she said,

'I found it at the back of a drawer,' because she
didn't want to talk about the flat.

'Max hasn't changed much, has he?' said Jenny, and Jimmy agreed cheerfully.

'He always was a handsome so-and-so.'

Anni's expression must have shown what she felt because Jenny said, 'Don't you think so?'

Anni shrugged and admitted, 'Not my type.'

But she had proof that an awful lot of women did fancy him. None of her workmates knew that Anni knew him. When she'd told them in the office about the city under the sea she had said that a friend was diving there, and that was true—Jimmy Stapleton had been Roger's friend.

She hadn't even mentioned knowing Torba twelve months before when they had run a survey in the magazine to find 'The man you would most like to be cast away with on a desert island' and he had headed the list.

The reasons readers gave were that he could cope with any emergency, would be able to build a boat or a hut, to catch and cook food. But most of all, of course that he was all man and guaranteed to turn the tropical nights into sizzling orgies.

Anni had disagreed emphatically, but she'd been the only girl on the staff who had.

'Hey,' said Jenny. 'Isn't that the man we saw earlier over there? Is he your type?'

It was Pete, sitting on a bar stool, and Anni wondered if he had come in here by chance or if she had been right once or twice when she had glimpsed him again in the narrow streets of the old town and wondered if he was following her. She hoped he was not, and she said, 'So it is.'

Philippe was looking their way now. Max was

playing some sort of board game with the grey-haired café owner, and Anni beckoned Philippe to come over and join her table. There was a seat by her and this seemed to be the livelier company.

When Max strolled across some time later Philippe was sitting with an arm resting along the back of Anni's chair, laughing and trying to talk her down.

Over delicious food they had somehow got round to the worst meal they could remember, capping each other's horrors. Anni had said that home cooking gone wrong was hard to beat for disaster if you were trying to impress. She had once given a dinner party, mixing salt for sugar in the *pièce de résistance*. Philippe said he knew the recipe, he'd come across it more than once. But if Anni had dished it up he would have eaten it—what man would not?

'Those that were at my dinner table,' said Anni. 'They all rounded on me as if I were poisoning them,' and it was hard to go on smiling with Max Torba standing just behind her. She didn't have to turn round to sense his presence and she wouldn't be telling any more silly stories while he was listening.

They were shifting seats to make room for him round the table when he said, 'Anni must see the kitchens.'

'Must I?'

'Of course. And compliment them on the *börek*—they're the speciality of the house.'

He stood back, waiting for her to get up and go with him, and she wanted to say no. It seemed to her there was a clash of wills for a moment, but what reason could she give for refusing to look at the kitchens, except that she wanted to stay here with friends around her?

She pushed back her chair and he went a few paces ahead, towards an archway leading from the courtyard. As she passed Pete she smiled vaguely in his direction and in the little passageway Max Torba turned. A couple of steps and she was up to him and she asked, 'Are the kitchens down here?' because he seemed to be blocking the way.

'The kitchens can wait,' he said, and she knew that her instinct was right, she should not have followed him because he looked grim and this was not going to be pleasant, 'while I brief you on the status of the men in the party.'

'What status?' She was bewildered. 'What are you talking about?'

'Philippe is married with two children. Henry has a live-in girlfriend and a wedding planned, and Jen and Jimmy are a working and loving partnership. I am not having you stirring up anything to amuse yourself.'

He saw her as a man-eater and a marriage wrecker and that was so absurd that she could only gasp, 'Do you think I could?'

'It's not beyond the bounds of possibility. They didn't meet you when you were eighteen so they'll take you at face-value.'

A couple of waiters came down the passage, bearing trays and singing out what was probably the Turkish for 'excuse me', but Anni hardly saw them. She had her back to the wall with Max Torba looking down at her, his dark eyes raking her, and she stared up at him unblinkingly because she would not for the world let him know how sick she felt.

She had been eighteen, a month before half a dozen friends went skiing together, when Roger brought Max Torba to their home for the first and last time for a New Year's Eve party in the riverside house in Henley where Anni had lived all her life. The new year had been welcomed in and they were still dancing and drinking and making merry, and Anni could hardly believe how pretty she looked. She was dancing with Robert and it was hard to believe that not so long before she had thought it heaven to be in his arms.

He had danced her out of the house into the cold bright night, where others were dancing under the stars, and the frozen grass crackled under their feet. By the mulberry tree he tried to kiss her and she let him and then she said, 'You're not very good at kissing, you know—not much of a turn-on. Ever thought of losing some weight? Underneath all this there could be quite a sexy feller. Not smart, but possibly sexy.'

He had gasped in shamefaced fashion, as well he might having once used much the same words to her, and she said as he had said, 'On your way, sweetie, you're beginning to bore me.'

She was dizzy with champagne and excitement that night, and as Robert slunk off across the lawn she leaned back against the tree and laughed softly, and that was when Max Torba walked round the tree.

'You're a brat pack all on your own, aren't you?' he said. 'When you grow up you're going to make one hell of a bitch.'

He had no right to judge her when he knew nothing about anything. She watched him walking away and wished she had the courage to shout after him, 'Don't call me a bitch, you bastard.' But she knew he would laugh at her and she hoped then that she might never have to see him again.

Of course he had remembered. So had she, but she had been trying to forget how she had disliked him to the point of loathing and now he was saying, 'Not that you look much older now. If anything the years have improved your looks.'

And that wasn't a compliment, he wasn't too pleased about that. 'If you put your mind to it some men might find it hard to resist you, so no games while you're here, you understand?'

That flicked her on the raw and she smiled a slow, feline smile. 'Not even if I promise not to play with your team? You think they might cheat, do you? Can't be trusted not to break the rules?' She thought she saw a muscle twitch near his cheekbone. It might have been shadow but it spurred her on and her voice was silky with malice. 'We can't have that, can we? But don't worry because I've got my own playmate, a very good friend. I usually travel with a friend—you never know when you might need one.'

She was still in the short shift dress but she managed to swish out of the passage like an angry cat, and she went straight over to Pete Hartley. When she reached him he detached himself from a group, moving along with her to the end of the bar.

'I'm flattered,' he said. 'You've left the great Max Torba to come over and talk to me.'

'I would leave Max Torba to come over and talk to a lampost,' she snapped. 'He was my brother's friend, not mine, although I do seem to be staying in his house.'

Pete's eyebrows rose. 'That can't be bad. It's quite a place.'

She agreed. 'And the others are nice.'

'Here he comes,' said Pete, and again without turning she was conscious of Max Torba just behind her. He couldn't be throwing a shadow, it had to be vibes, because even without Pete's warning she knew when he was close enough to touch her.

He did not touch her. He said, 'Hello,' and she had to turn her head. 'Introduce us,' he said.

'This is Pete Hartley, he's an up-and-coming actor. And surprise, surprise, Pete, this is the one and only Max Torba.'

She expected Pete to take his cue from her flip tone and say something like, 'But of course it is, who else?' but instead he said, 'How d'you do? This is a great pleasure,' with an enthusiasm that did not seem to be acting.

'Thank you,' replied Max. 'It's good to meet any friend of Anni's.'

You hypocrite, she thought. Although he probably was glad to meet somebody he thought was her lover.

'She'll have told you she's staying at the villa,' said Max. 'Why don't you move in too? You could share Anni's room.'

CHAPTER THREE

'How kind,' said Anni crisply.

Max repied, 'Not at all.'

Pete was still at a loss for words as Max walked away, and Anni said, 'Forget it, he's got the wrong idea. I might have suggested just now that we were old mates. I did not say bedmates but that seems to be how his mind works.'

'So does mine.' Pete was still grinning when Max reached the others. Anni wondered what he was telling them because they all looked her way and Pete was wheedling, 'I've heard it's a big house, isn't there a little room I could have?'

'You mean free board and lodging?' It was bad enough being indebted to Max Torba for those herself, she was not taking along any hangers-on. She said, 'We'll see if the offer stands when I tell him you picked me up last night and all I know about you is what you've told me.'

'When you know me better, perhaps I can take up his offer,' he said hopefully.

'Not for sharing my room.' They were all smiling at her. Max must have told them that Pete was her very good friend, and she said, 'I didn't realise you were a Torba fan.'

'I've never met him before, but he's a powerful writer and he's got a lot of clout. I wouldn't mind getting into the Torba circle. What have you got against him?'

She gestured helplessly. 'Too big, too success-ful, but boy does he have his fans.'

'Got his enemies too. He writes some hard-hitting stuff. For every fifty fans there's got to be one who's gunning for him.'

'Good,' she said. 'I could be in at the kill. Think what a scoop that would be for me.'

Of course she was fooling, and so was Pete; they laughed together. Across the room the others were getting up from their tables, as it was time to leave, and Pete asked, 'Where will you be tomorrow?'

'I'm going to see what's going on with the diving.'

'I'll be there.'

She wouldn't mind that. 'Come over and say hello to them,' she said.

They were waiting to meet him; everybody was very affable. Pete apologised to Max. 'About your invitation—thanks a lot, I do appreciate it, but right now I've booked in down here.'

'He likes the bright lights,' Anni said gaily.

'A pity,' said Max, smiling. 'I hoped you'd keep Anni in order.'

As if she were still the brat he had called her all those years ago! Pete was laughing and saying, 'I'll try.'

'Don't bank on it, bigger men than you have failed,' Anni quipped back with the first wisecrack to come into her head. If she had stopped to think she would not have mentioned bigger men. 'See you tomorrow,' she said, and Pete put an arm around her as he went with them all into the road where the car was parked.

Outside Anni shrugged him away and hissed out of the corner of her mouth, 'Don't push your luck.' When he tried to kiss her goodnight she turned her head so that his lips slid across her cheek, and hopped briskly into the back of the car.

'Well, tell us about him,' said Jen, waving as Pete waved goodbye from the pavement, and Anni reeled off what Pete had told her about himself last night.

'Well, he's an actor. He's done some TV ads and a few plays. Fringe companies, festivals, off Broadway. Expecting his big break any day now, you know how it is.'

'He's pretty,' Jenny said. 'Didn't you want to bring him along?'

'I think I can make it through the night without him,' Anni replied drily.

When they reached the villa they were ready for their beds. Next morning it would be breakfast at eight and then down to the bay, with Anni going along as an observer.

'Come and see,' Henry said, and they went into the room on the ground floor that had been given over to the city under the sea. The walls were papered with maps, drawings, underwater and aerial photographs. Finds—pieces of pottery, a stone anchor, part of a statue—had been photographed and then handed over. And every

summer the team came back, following the ruins
a little further.

Anni was enthralled. She answered, 'Goodnight,' mechanically as they drifted off, and stood
for a long time staring at a big survey map with
enough streets marked out for you to begin to
imagine the shape of the ancient town.

'So long ago,' she murmured.

Beside her Max asked, 'What did you do about
the apartment?'

She spun round, jerked from her reverie, realising for the first time that they had all gone but
him. He was asking about Roger's flat and she
had a question about something that had been
puzzling her. 'They don't know anything about it,
do they? You didn't even mention it to Jimmy.
Didn't you think he might have been interested?'

Instead of answering he asked again, 'What did
you do about it?'

'Nothing yet.' She had mentioned it to no one,
nor had she contacted the folk on the photograph.
'Why didn't you tell Jimmy?'

He said quietly, 'Because as soon as it becomes
common knowledge you're going to be harassed,
and not just by those who knew Roger. You're a
journalist, you know a human interest story, the
tabloids would love it. You might not mind, but it
is your business and you might prefer to keep it
that way.'

Of course, an apartment locked up for nearly a
decade, everything as it was left by a young man
about to die, would cause a stir. His sister, who'd
had no idea what she was going to find until she

turned the key she had inherited, would be hounded out of her mind.

She knew that and she had shrunk from the prospect. She also knew nobody else would have kept quiet without even being asked. Under heavy lids Max Torba's eyes told nothing, the sensual mouth was close-lipped, and it was ironic that the man she had never trusted should also be a man you could trust.

She said, 'You're right. Thank you.' She might end up telling nobody else, cleaning it out herself. She almost asked, 'What would you do about it?' but she mustn't turn to him for advice. For a long time now she had made her own decisions, and it must be remembering old days that was making her suddenly insecure.

'It's a big place you've got there,' she said, nodding towards the map on the wall.

'We haven't got it,' he denied emphatically. 'The team have permission to dive, but they'd lose it fast enough if they got any delusions about ownership.'

'Yes, of course.' She knew that. 'Goodnight, then,' she said, and she came out into the big room and walked up the stairs.

Lights still burned and behind closed doors the others were getting ready for bed. There were staff here too, but the house seemed silent. Her sandals made a flapping noise on the polished boards, soft as following footsteps, and at the end of the corridor she turned and looked back. There was no one there and everything looked different in daylight.

It was a rambling old villa and she would sound such an idiot if she had to go downstairs again and tell Max Torba, 'I've lost my way. Do you happen to know which room she put me in?'

He might even, heaven forbid, think she was being flirtatious. He thought she was chatting up the men in the party and having an affair with Pete, but he must know she would never be stupid enough to believe he might find her attractive.

She shrugged impatiently, shaking sense back into her head, and almost at once she recognised the pattern of a wall carpet and remembered that her room was just along the corridor.

The clear water was turquoise-green with dark blue shadows and Anni was longing to slip down into its cool depths. She had been fascinated with everything she had seen up to now. She had been shown around the launch by the brothers who crewed it, and she had admired it all from the gallery to the wheelhouse. She had met most of the students who were camping in the tents, and been presented to Yusef Guzel, the Turkish expert on nautical antiquities, a big, booming, jolly man with a lot of curly hair and moustachios.

From the launch the divers went down, working within the section marked out by bobbing buoys, and in the saloon they pieced together the data of the day. They all had their equipment and their tasks. They were all busy. Except Anni, who finally found herself leaning over the rail looking down into the water, and Max, who seemed to have come along for the ride.

He was reading a newspaper, sitting in a canvas-backed chair, the sun beating down on his thatch of dark hair and his broad mahogany-tanned shoulders. She wondered what today's headlines were, but he seemed absorbed and she couldn't see herself sidling up and trying to start a conversation.

She watched the others and, when Jimmy came up the boarding ladder from the dinghy, unstrapping his harness, she asked, 'Is it all right if I go in?'

'Sure,' said Jimmy, and Max looked across.

'You can swim, I suppose?'

Anni said, 'No. I thought I'd just jump and see if I float.'

Obviously the water was deep and there might be rocks and reefs, but she was not lunatically reckless and he said, 'Of course you can, and of course you can take care of yourself, so why do I feel that somebody should be keeping an eye on you?'

'Because she's Roger's kid sister,' said Jimmy sentimentally, and Anni thought how cosy that sounded coming from Jimmy, and how uncomfortable she felt with Max Torba's eyes on her.

She had brought a swimsuit and she went below, slipping out of the dress, bra and pants in a little cabin. Then she came up on deck and dived from the rail. If he was watching he couldn't fault that dive. She went in with hardly a splash, grinning with closed lips.

The water felt wonderful but she was skimming

the surface. Holding her breath, she could only stay under briefly, not far enough down to see anything but brightly coloured fish. Silver trails of rising bubbles pin-pointed the divers far below and she swam around, gulping in air, doing a series of duck dives and coming up with bursting lungs and mounting frustration.

It was all happening down there. Well, not much was actually happening—this was a slow and painstaking operation—but that was where the city was, in the blue darkness, and she desperately wanted to see.

After a while she swam back to the dinghy and clambered aboard, then climbed up the ladder. Up here Philippe squatted on the deck, his camera beside him, and Max was still behind his newspaper.

Anni pushed back her dripping hair and begged, 'Please, is there any chance of my going down? I have done open-water scuba diving.'

Philippe didn't say no, he seemed to be considering it, and when she looked at Max she read his expression as, You can sink without trace for all I care. 'Where?' he asked.

'Where did I dive? I took a course with the British Subaqua Club for a series called "Try Something New". I loved it.'

'Get into the gear,' he said.

He wasn't in charge. It was his launch but it was not his expedition, yet he was giving the orders. Although she supposed a good way to check her would be to see how she handled the equipment. If she fumbled she was a beginner, and then they could say no go.

She had done well on the course. She knew how to kit herself up, but with Max Torba watching her every move her fingers could turn into thumbs, so she looked away from him as she fixed the webbing harness of her backpack over her shoulders and checked the rubber tubes with gauges and regulators.

She tested a face mask for fit, doing it all in a methodical, unhurried fashion, and when she did glance his way he was waiting, fully kitted, even to a knife in his belt.

'You're coming in with me?' That dismayed her. She knew they wouldn't let her go down alone, but she would have preferred anyone to him. 'Aren't you busy?' she asked lamely.

'I'm the only one who isn't. After you down the ladder.' In the dinghy as she put on fins he said, 'Stay close,' and she took out her mouthpiece to snap at him.

'You stay close, I didn't ask you to come.' Then she slipped into the water, holding the mask to her face and jumping in feet first and together, clearing her ears and her mask as she descended.

Why *had* she said that? It was so childish. But she had been longing to swim down and see what was happening, and having him near would spoil everything, like a shadow taking the sunshine away. The sunshine had faded now into bright green water above and they were floating down, feet first, into another world where fronds of weeds moved like trees in a gentle breeze and black and yellow fish darted like birds.

When her feet touched the seabed Max was almost face to face with her and she released compressed air until she had enough buoyancy to swim around. She didn't look for him. Any time she got lost she could fin her way up to the surface and she would pretend she was alone.

But he was swimming beside her. He turned when she turned, staying with her so that she couldn't avoid seeing him and noticing that he had a marvellous body, the muscles smooth and rippling. He swam with a lazy ease, and with eye mask and mouthpiece he might not have been Max Torba at all.

He could be someone she was meeting for the first time in an alien land. Or he could be Torba transformed by 'a sea change into something rich and strange'. Except that Max Torba always had been rich and strange so that wouldn't be much of a change.

And even through eye masks in the dim blue light she felt that she could have recognised his eyes, and his hair and his hands and all of him as if she had known his body as well as she knew her own.

Then he touched her hand and pointed to the shadowy shape of a great fish. Lord, she thought, a shark? She clutched his fingers convulsively. But the fish passed below them and a shoal of smaller fish was swimming unpanicked so it couldn't have been a shark.

If it had been, she thought, you're the one I'd

have wanted with me; and after that it was fantastic. He took her through a slow, strange, sensuous
world where there were marvellous things to see
and every rock had its own weird beauty.
Although she saw nothing that looked like the
remains of a city.

She couldn't really have expected walls and
buildings. An earthquake had submerged it and
the seas of two thousand years had pounded over
it. It was a miracle that anything was left. But then
he beckoned her and she saw a long, flat stone.
And another set straight beyond it, and beyond
that a line of stones vanishing in the dark water.

She swam closer, touching the stones, following
them, and although the line soon broke it was
obviously man-made. This would have been the
edge of a street, maybe the main road, and she
remembered the plan of the city and felt the thrill
of discovery. If she had been on land she would
have danced for joy and she did do a little excited
twirl.

After that she watched avidly, scared of missing
anything, and Max took her to other rocks and
stones where the weeds had been cleared and
markers set, and she ran wondering fingers over
them. He talked to her with gestures, making the
outline of an archway, a pillar, a row of buildings,
and she played the game with the zest of someone
who was well and truly hooked. As she read the
clues she 'saw' the city rising from the ruins.

They came across none of the others; he was
probably keeping her away from the working area
in case she stirred up sand or disturbed anyone.

But this was much better than swimming carefully among the scientific equipment of a marine expedition.

Exploring, roaming free as a fish, was a voyage of incredible discovery. And there was danger in it. In places the weeds grew thick, but she avoided the waving branches and he carried a knife, so that only gave her a little thrill of fear that sharpened her senses even more.

Once she was scared. They were swimming a few feet above the sea bed when suddenly it fell away in a vertical drop. She could only guess at the depth but the water was pitch-black down there. It must be hundreds of feet deep and she couldn't see the other side. It was like a black hole in space that had sunk to the sea bed, and instinctively she held back as if she would drop like a stone if she went further.

He turned and waved her to follow and she closed her eyes and then he was beside her and they swam on together. She kept close by him, looking down apprehensively because anything could lurk in those depths, and then just as suddenly the sea bed reappeared beneath them. You are the first man, she thought, I've followed over the edge of a cliff, and held-down laughter made her shoulders shake.

She had checked her gauges when he did, always surprised at how fast her air tank seemed to be emptying, how quickly time must be passing, and when he signalled up she wanted to plead for longer. But the air tanks were calling time and she went up, slowly and reluctantly,

facing him and wondering if she looked as woebe-
gone as she felt. It was like leaving a wonderful
place that you could never go back to and that
was sad, and stupid because of course she could
go back.

They surfaced together near to the launch and
Max pushed back his mask and said, 'I'm sorry it
wasn't Atlantis.'

'Oh, but it was,' she contradicted. 'I saw the tall
towers.'

He looked at her for a moment, then said with
a smile, 'I believe you did,' and she was sure that
he saw them too. She wanted to swim closer so
that she was in his arms, and then she heard her
name. Somebody was hollering 'Anni' and Max
drawled, 'Your very good friend seems to be
calling you.'

At the rail of the launch the sun was shining on
Pete's golden hair and Anni watched Max swim
away. He didn't look back for her, and why
should he? He knew she was a good swimmer
and Pete was waiting for her. She swam slowly
with the hot sun on her and thought wryly, Why
is it that the men who are waiting for me are
usually the Petes of this world?

Pete was waiting for her at the top of the ladder.
When he reached for her she told him, 'I couldn't
be wetter, you'll get soaked.'

'Who cares? I thought I'd lost you. I've been
here for hours.'

You couldn't lose what you'd never had, and
everyone knew she was safe with Max. She said,

'Then there's something wrong with your watch, because I haven't been gone for hours.'

There were more of them on deck now and she began telling them how much she had enjoyed herself, making them all smile at her bubbling enthusiasm. Getting out of the gear, she shook the drops of water from her and Pete picked up her suntan oil and asked, 'Shall I oil you?'

She would burn in this heat with no protection but the briefest of swimsuits, and she said, 'I'll change, and I've got a hat and my sunglasses in the cabin.'

She held out her hand for the bottle which he seemed unwilling to let go, and hurried down the steps because Pete was following her. He really fancied himself, but if he thought he was lounging in the doorway while she stripped off he had another think coming.

She shut the cabin door, pushing the bolt to, and immediately there was a tap. She called, 'Go away, Pete, you are not required,' and peeled off her swimsuit, borrowing a towel to mop herself dry and rub her wet hair.

Then she began to oil herself, stretching to reach between her shoulder-blades, covering every-where so that Pete would have no excuse to say, 'You've missed a bit—here, let me.' She did not want Pete's hands on her, not even being helpful with the sun oil.

Running her fingers down the slippery length of her leg, she found herself thinking of Max, wondering what his touch would be like. When he'd swum beside her, beckoned to her, guided her, it had been as though they floated touching everywhere. And she wondered what it would be like to lie with him here, in this little cabin, sharing each other's warmth.

Her thoughts staggered her so that she nearly dropped the greasy bottle. What was she thinking of? The man and the city had both been mirages. She knew all about the rapture of the deep, where divers saw mermaids and monsters and lost all sense of reality. But that was when their oxygen was failing. There was no excuse for her, and she scrambled to get clothes over her shining nakedness.

She put on sunglasses and they slid down her nose. She saw her startled eyes staring from a small wall mirror, and dabbed the bridge of her nose with the end of the towel to reduce the oil slip. That was better. They were big glasses and they hid most of her face, and she pulled a small grimace trying to see the funny side, because on land Max Torba's touch was something she would run to avoid.

If he did touch her it would be a grip on her arm, or a tap on her shoulder because she was straying out of step. He thought she was a pest. He had taken her diving as he would have taken any journalist who could scuba dive and was interested in the city. Of course it didn't mean that he fancied her, and anyhow she was back to normal now.

Pete was waiting outside the cabin and she said, 'You ought to go down. It's like another planet down there.'

'Not for me,' said Pete. 'Did you find any buried treasure? Didn't Torba find you a pearl? I should have thought he could find them with his eyes closed with his luck. This is some boat he's got. Nothing but the best, eh?'

'That's the way of it,' said Anni lightly. She had begrudged Max Torba's success for years, but that bitterness had only hurt herself, and she went into the saloon to look again at the photographs and the maps. Pete didn't seem enthusiastic but Anni had her articles to write.

The saloon was deserted except for one student, sitting at a table frowning over notes he was making. Anni said, 'Hello, how goes it?' and got a blank stare. When she smiled he half smiled and bent his head over his work again.

She showed Pete the map and talked about the city, and they looked at the sketches including the head and torso of a marble faun. It must have been a glorious day when they brought that up, and there was an underwater photograph of it half buried in the sands, and a photograph of Henry surfacing, cradling it in his arms. She said, 'Everything has to be handed over, of course. Mind you,' she paused and Pete cocked an enquiring eyebrow, 'if Max Torba took a fancy to something I shouldn't be surprised if it got smuggled out.'

She was joking and Pete was grinning. 'He could have cellars back home stacked with the stuff,' she gurgled, 'because he isn't overburdened with scruples.'

'I wouldn't put it past him,' said Pete.

They were down below for about ten minutes and when they came up on deck there was a picnic going on. They were all sitting around, drinking cold drinks, eating fruit or forking up buffet food from plastic plates.

Max stood by the ladder talking to Yusef, and when Anni and Pete emerged he looked across at them and Anni felt a hot blush scalding her cheeks. She was carrying her swimsuit, bare-legged and wearing a mini-skirted dress, oiled from head to foot, and beside her Pete, as usual, was grinning.

She wanted to say, 'I locked the door on him. We haven't been down there in a cabin together.'

That was what they all thought had been happening and nobody cared anyway—certainly Max did not. She was imagining that his expression was wry as he turned back to Yusef and almost immediately climbed down the ladder into the dinghy.

'Come and have something to eat,' Jenny called. 'We're through diving for the day.'

The dinghy, with Max aboard, was drawing away and Anni went to the rail, asking anybody, 'Where's Max going?'

'Back to the villa,' said Henry.

She didn't want to be left on the launch. She would rather go back to the villa and walk round the gardens or maybe start writing up her notes. She almost called over the water, 'Please come back and take me with you.' But then she bit her lip because what she really wanted was just to go with him, while the last thing he would want would be to get lumbered with her.

She took the glass of iced orange juice that Jenny was offering her and went to join them and wait until they all took the dinghy back to shore.

That wasn't for hours. They were discussing everything that had happened this morning, and then they sunbathed, sprawled out on deck, and Anni joined in the general chatter, while most of the time Pete snored gently beside her.

From time to time she dozed herself, woken from one siesta when Pete kissed her and breathed hotly on her cheek, 'Wake up, sleeping beauty.'

She sat up, swaying away from him, yawning and saying, 'Don't tell me my prince has come.'

Jenny laughed. 'Not only that but your carriage awaits. We're through for the day. Coming?'

Anni grabbed her bag and Pete asked plaintively, 'Can I tag along?'

'Go back to Idessa,' Anni hissed. Once he got up to the villa he would be angling for another invitation to stay there and he was not using her as a meal ticket.

'You're a hard-hearted woman,' he whispered in her ear. 'Where do we meet tomorrow? Here?'

'I don't know what I'll be doing.'

'I'll wait at our table for you.'

'You do that.'

She had no plans for tomorrow. She would see what tomorrow brought. By now she almost felt like one of the team, they had accepted her so readily. Tonight they were having their meal at the villa, spending the evening together, and when she walked into her bedroom she was really looking forward to the hours ahead.

She heard the typewriter, so Max was working again in his room nearby. She wondered if he had climbed up the steep hillside and thought he had; the car was standing where they had left it this morning. The heat didn't seem to bother him. He wouldn't have reached the gates as she had, pouring sweat and croaking for water.

She didn't look much better now, with her hair lank and greasy, but before she went downstairs again tonight she would take some time and trouble. Most of the clothes she had packed for coming here were cotton, but she had silk shirts and a couple of silk dresses, all clean, unfussy lines. She usually looked elegant. One of her friends had once sighed, 'Anni could get away with wearing a dustbin liner.'

Anni had laughed and said, 'You should have seen me in my teens when I was the shape of a dustbin.'

It would be very informal tonight. The model-girl image would be wildly out of place, but with the minimum of make-up and a crisp white cotton dress cinched with a wide belt round her narrow waist she shouldn't look too bad.

She showered and washed her hair and made notes on the day, without once mentioning Max, although she sat thinking about him. The old resentment had gone and in its place was an anticipation that made her eyes sparkle.

She was here for a while and she would show him that she was a brat no longer. There had been

rapport while they were diving, and if Pete hadn't
turned up they would have swum back together
and gone on talking, she was almost sure of it. So
that when Max had come back to the villa she
might have asked if she could go too. Anyhow,
starting tonight, she wouldn't put a foot wrong.

The faint sound of the typewriter had stopped
for good this time it seemed. She had been aware
of the pause, waiting to hear it start up again, but
for quite a while there had been silence. 'We eat
around seven,' Jenny had told her, and it was
half-past six now so she had been sitting here
daydreaming for the best part of an hour, and she
set about her make-up with a light touch.

She didn't need a blusher. The sun had caught
her, making her skin glow. Her hair fell casually,
short and beautifully cut—she had a super hair-
dresser at home—and her eyes seemed brighter
than usual. Not bad, she thought, not bad at all;
she found herself touching wood with crossed
fingers, and laughed at herself for hoping that
Max would like the way she looked.

The main salon was uncluttered and spacious,
with white walls and marble floor, but the dining-
room leading off was rather splendid. Oyster-
coloured silk covered the walls and the wall hang-
ings and carpets were in deep jewel colours. The
long dining table was in black marble, shining like
a mirror, and the black carved high-backed chairs
were upholstered in garnet-red brocade. The wine
glasses were in red and green Venetian glass and
Anni, who usually preferred white wine, chose

red because it looked gorgeous in the deep red goblet.

The food was delicious, the main course a chicken dish in an incredible creamy sauce that tasted of garlic, paprika and walnuts, topped with walnut halves. When Anni said, 'This is out of this world, does it have a name?' Jenny told her,

'Circassian chicken. Brought to Istanbul by slave girls from the Caucassus, guaranteed to pep up the appetite of the sultan. In those days it took hours to get the walnut paste smooth, so it had to be a labour of love.'

'Wow,' said Anni and she turned to Max, wide eyes sparkling. 'Who pounds your walnuts?'

'Sezer,' he said, 'with a blender.'

'Ah,' she sighed, 'I thought you might have a slave girl tucked away.'

'They're not so easy to come by these days.' He grinned.

'Don't look at me,' she said in mock horror. She ate another morsel and sighed again, blissfully this time. 'But it is delicious.' She looked around at all of them and said impulsively, 'Oh, this is *nice*.'

'Isn't it?' Henry spoke for them all. 'We really look forward to coming here every year. Mags comes over too—she's my lady—and Philippe's family come and it's always brilliant.'

'We found it, you know,' said Jenny triumphantly. 'Jimmy and I on our honeymoon. Max lent us the villa and we were following up clues, but we never thought we'd find ruins right here in this bay. It always seemed too good to be true, one of those amazing breaks that make you believe in magic. Every year, every summer we come. You could make it a date too.' She looked at Max archly. 'Couldn't she?'

'Of course,' he said, and, although he could hardly say anything else, Anni thought, Oh, I wish I could!

She said, 'Thank you,' and after that she sat back and listened to them talking. She noticed how little Max said in comparison to the rest. He didn't chatter at all, he just put in the occasional word that kept the conversation going. The rest of the time he seemed to be giving them his attention, but she wondered what he was thinking. He was a secretive man, deep as the black hole on the sea bed.

But as she met his eyes over the dinner table it seemed that everyone else faded away, that he called her name and reached her soul. Her heart was pounding faster and louder, then she heard Jimmy's faraway voice asking, 'Who would that be?' and realised that the beat was not inside her.

Someone was knocking hard on a door, and through the open door into the big room Anni saw Sezer's husband hurrying past. He was a wiry, small-framed man and the three men who came with him were all young and taller. Without giving him a chance to speak one pushed ahead, elbowing him aside, and stood flanked by his companions—three men in green battledress with rifles slung.

Max got up, asking, '*Ne istiyor musunuz?*' which had to mean, What do you want?

Revolution? thought Anni. Are we hostages?

Nobody was shouting and, apart from the rifles, they didn't seem threatening. The one in the middle, the officer, looked boyish and rather embarrassed. He talked rapidly, waving and shrugging. Max spoke little and calmly. Then he led the way out of the room and the three intruders followed him.

'What's happening?' Anni croaked.

They all seemed to have been struck dumb, but Jimmy gasped, 'Lord knows.'

'Is that the army?'

'The *jandarma*.' She knew that meant the police. 'The uniform hasn't changed since they were chasing mountain bandits.'

'What do the police want?' Anni persisted.

Jenny said, 'It's all right, hon. Nothing to do with you. You stay here.' But as they hurried out Anni followed them and almost at once Max came out of the 'city' room, still striding a pace or two ahead, and led the *jandarma* through a door that led down to the cellars.

Anni hung back. She had no idea what was going on but she knew they would resent her bothering them with any more questions. They stood in a hushed group and the tension was electric.

When the four men came up from the cellars nobody else was speaking but Max and the officer. Max accompanied them to the open front door, like a host bidding guests goodbye, standing there until Anni heard the sounds of a vehicle being driven away, and a moment or two longer until, presumably, it was out of the gates.

Then he came back, closing the door behind him, and it was Jimmy who asked, 'What the hell was that about? What sparked that off?'

'You gathered, didn't you?' A worried murmur answered him. Anni, it seemed, was the only one who didn't understand the language. 'They've had information that finds are being withheld.'

'Bloody rubbish!' Henry exploded. 'Yusef knows that, he's been with us from the beginning. He knows we wouldn't be daft enough to bend the rules.'

Max said, 'They couldn't get hold of him. They will tomorrow but, when the officer's cousin made the report, that got action. He was civil about it but the launch and the house could be under supervision from now on. And heaven help any of us when we go through the Customs.'

A groan went up. Jenny was almost in tears. 'It's the beginning of the end, isn't it? They're going to ban us. This has got to be just an excuse because nothing has gone out, *nothing*.'

Max drawled, 'That wasn't what the officer's cousin said.

'Who is this officer's cousin?' demanded Philippe.

'A student,' said Max, watching Anni and every word terrified her, 'who was in the saloon on the launch today and heard somebody say I had cellars stuffed with loot. He's satisfied himself there's nothing but wine down these cellars but he suspects I could be crating it out.'

Anni's hand was pressed to her mouth and Max said grimly, 'It's too late for that, you should have been gagged from birth.'

They were all staring at her now. 'Anni?' Jenny whispered. 'You never said that?'

Anni's voice was muffled, her hand still over her mouth. 'I didn't mean it. It was a joke.'

'You always did have a warped sense of humour.'

Max couldn't have looked grimmer, and wildly she tried to explain, repeating, 'I was joking. With Pete. I didn't know anyone else overheard. That student, I didn't think he understood.'

He had not replied to her because he had not wanted to talk. He was busy with his work, a serious young man with a cousin in the *jandarma*. She had no excuse and Jimmy said, as if he couldn't believe it, 'You made that kind of accusation in front of a witness? Didn't you know it was dynamite?'

Of course she knew. And Max had told her their permission to dive would end if anything soured the good relationship. Henry was shaking his head, saying, 'I can't credit anybody being this thick. A kid of five would have more gumption. How old are you?'

'Twenty-six, going on a backward eighteen,' said Max scathingly. 'You haven't changed much since then, have you? You still don't give a damn for the trouble you cause.' And he sounded as if he wished he had never set eyes on her.

CHAPTER FOUR

'SHALL I leave?' asked Anni.

'Don't tempt me,' said Max harshly. 'It would be a pleasure to throw you out on the mountainside.' She might as well be out there as in here with him, because he looked as dangerous as anything that prowled in the night. 'But unfortunately I'll need you in the morning to explain your idea of a joke.'

How she was going to do that she could not imagine, but she said, 'Of course I will. And Pete will back me up. It's got to be all right.'

Nobody took any notice of her futile reassurance. Philippe asked, 'Will they be back?'

'Probably,' said Max.

'Searching here?'

'Possibly.'

'Max,' Jenny sounded as if another problem had just occurred to her, 'what about your papers? You won't want anyone rooting through them.'

'They don't refer to the city,' Max said. 'In any case, they won't get them.'

'But——' Jenny was beginning again when Jimmy hushed her.

'Honey, watch it.' He looked hard-eyed at Anni and she knew that she was the eavesdropper who couldn't be trusted.

Again she said miserably, 'I was joking.'

'You could have got Max arrested!' Henry roared at her. 'You still could, you stupid cow. He could be in a Turkish gaol tomorrow, and we can kiss the city goodbye. Take it from me, kiddo, nobody's laughing; this is no joke.'

'It had better be,' said Max drily, 'because that's our story and we're sticking to it.' As Anni tried to stammer something he said with a contempt that shrivelled her, 'Go upstairs and rehearse your piece. It shouldn't be hard to convince the authorities that you're the original birdbrain.'

They were all talking but Max as she ran up the stairs, and their shrill voices seemed to follow her down the corridors until she clapped her hands over her ears, almost stumbling into her bedroom where she sat huddled on the side of her bed for a long time.

She was desperately sorry for the team. With a few careless words she could have banished them from their little paradise, and was Henry right? Could Max be arrested on nothing more than something silly that someone had said?

Surely not when there was no scrap of proof. But it was still a thought that brought a rush of horrific images to mind until she was frantically comforting herself, telling herself, He'll handle it, Max won't let it get out of hand.

They were all ranting and raving but him. He was quiet and steady as a rock. As angry with her as the rest, but with the strength to keep control no matter what happened, and tomorrow the situation would be defused. Although nobody would forget it.

As soon as she had done all she could to make amends she would have to leave here. She had wanted things to be different. It had seemed like a wonderful beginning but it had ended miserably and there was nothing she could do about that.

She crept in and out of the bathroom before anyone else came up. Downstairs they would be talking and talking, and up here she was supposed to be thinking about how she was going to explain to the authorities. But what could she tell them except that what she said on the launch had meant nothing and she was sorry she had said it?

Her reflection before she went down this evening had pleased her, and she had thought Max might realise that she was a sexy-looking girl, but she didn't look sexy now, and the only joy he wanted from her was the pleasure of throwing her out.

What a stupid, crazy muddle it all was! She kicked the waste-paper basket across the room and beat on the pillow with clenched fists because she was so furious with herself.

And, of course, she passed a restless night. Sometimes when she woke she thought, I can make them understand it's all a fuss about nothing, and drifted back into an uneasy slumber. More often she remembered Jenny wailing, 'They're going to ban us,' and Henry shouting, 'He could be in gaol tomorrow,' and lay tossing and turning and worrying herself sick.

In the morning she waited until the last minute before she went down. She was going to improve nobody's appetite and she wanted no breakfast herself. In the end Sezer was sent to call her, rapping on the door with all the smiling wrinkles in her face clenched tight with disapproval.

'I'll be right down,' said Anni. 'I suppose you don't speak English? I thought that lad didn't and that was a mistake, but I see you know how things stand and you don't think it was funny.'

She was talking to herself. Sezer had stomped off and Anni made her own way to the terrace, under a trellis of vine leaves, where they were all finishing breakfast. Yesterday she had been welcomed, but when she appeared this morning all the talking stopped.

'Coffee or tea?' said Max. Always the host, she thought. Nobody else would offer me anything, but speaking to me doesn't mean you've forgiven me any more than they have.

'Coffee, please,' she said, and helped herself.

Jenny slipped off her sunglasses and blew her nose. Her eyelids were puffy; she had been crying. She must be devastated by the threat of losing their diving permits and Anni said, 'Oh, Jenny, I am sorry.'

'Just shut up,' hissed Jenny.

'Keep this in proportion,' Max put in quietly. 'I'm sure it can be settled. What exactly did you say?'

His eyes seemed to bore into her skull and she answered jerkily, 'I—can't remember—word for word.'

'Oh, I'm sure you can. A journalist can't have less-than-a-day recall.' He paused and drawled, 'Although maybe in your case——'

Suddenly she felt anger prickling her nerve-ends. She hadn't meant to hurt anyone and she had just passed a wretched night worrying about them. About him most of all. Now he was goading her unmercifully. He might be tough as old boots, but she was falling apart, and if he wanted to hear exactly what she had said he should hear.

She looked him straight in the eyes and said, clearly and crisply, 'I was going round the saloon with Pete. Showing him the pictures and the maps. As I'm supposed to be writing about it I was looking at it all again. And I said,' she hesitated, then quoted herself without pausing or taking another breath, '"Everything has to be handed over, of course. Mind you, if Max Torba took a fancy to something I shouldn't be surprised if it got smuggled out. He could have cellars back home stacked with the stuff, because he isn't overburdened with scruples."'

They were shocked rigid. At first Max's face was masklike, then he actually seemed amused, and perhaps he was. 'Now there's a character reference that should stand me in good stead,' he said.

'That was your idea of a *joke*?' shrieked Jenny. 'We were laughing.'

She should not have repeated it and Max said wryly, 'The *jandarm's* cousin didn't seem to think so. He believed he was hearing proof of criminal conspiracy.'

Jimmy snarled at her, 'Don't say that again. Say you don't remember what you said. Max should sue you for slander.'

Nobody spoke to her on their way down the mountainside, and when the car drew up Yusef and Ali from the launch were waiting. Grim-faced, they were two different men from the affable characters of yesterday. Ali was here to tell Max that the launch had been gone over, but at least Yusef greeted Max like a brother in trouble, clapping him on the shoulder and shaking his hand.

Yusef Guzel's sympathies were with them, but when he looked towards Anni exasperation seemed to rise from him like steam and she said meekly, 'I never expected to be taken seriously.'

'Women!' he said, rolling his eyes, which would not please Jenny. He glowered at Anni while Max was telling him that nobody took any notice of her; he was talking in Turkish, but Anni knew she was being described as a feather-brained idiot and Yusef was agreeing with every word.

So were the others, they were all glaring at her, and when there was silence for a moment she ventured to ask, 'Could I go with you to the authorities, whoever they are, and make a statement?'

Yusef looked at Max, who said, 'I'd prefer it if she was kept well away. Her idea of a statement would probably make matters worse. She can't help babbling.'

She wanted to shout, 'I do not,' but she had to stand there like a scolded child while they went on talking and ignoring her, and when a crowded bus came bumping along the road she asked, without much hope, 'May I go, then?'

Yusef made a dismissing gesture that she took

to mean yes, and she ran for the bus. Every seat was taken and the aisle was full, but she clung on to a rail by the open doorway, swinging like a local. If she fell off, so long as she was out of sight it would do for now, but at the next stop two men with three sacks got out and she managed to squirm inside.

In Idessa Pete was sitting at the table where she had first met him, a half-empty glass of *raki* in front of him. He grinned when he saw her and she ordered a glass of fruit juice and took several gulps before she felt up to sharing her problem.

'You remember that student in the saloon yesterday when we were looking around? Well, he could understand English and he was listening while I was rabbiting on about Max Torba smuggling the finds out, and he's got a cousin in the police and last night the villa got raided.'

Pete choked on his *raki*. 'Did they find anything?'

'Of course they didn't.'

'Does Torba know who shopped him?'

'He surely does. I jumped on that bus to get away from him. He's being questioned and I'm praying it's going to be all right. They're diving on sufferance and they've been keeping a low profile for years; I could just have blown it for them. And the police could be coming back and tearing the place apart.'

'You still reckon they'll find nothing?'

'Nothing from the city, that's for sure, but he must have something that's pretty hot because he was saying nobody's getting hold of his papers.'

She drank deeply of her iced apricot juice and sighed.

'Cheer up, chicken, let's hit the road,' suggested Pete.

He had a motorbike and they rode into another busier town, exploring the market, visiting the ruins of some old Roman baths and a glittering golden mosque. It should all have been enjoyable but she couldn't stop wondering what would be waiting for her when she returned to Nidus. All day long Max Torba was never out of her mind. If he had been walking beside her she could not have been more acutely conscious of him, and at last she said, 'I have go to back now.'

'I've got a room here, how about staying with me? We could collect your luggage some time when he isn't around.' And Anni gave a little gurgle of laughter at the idea of moving into Pete's clutches.

'No, thanks,' she said. 'I've had a lovely day,' and that was a lie, 'but I do have to go now. Will you take me or shall I get a taxi?' And all the way, as the bike bounced over the hard, rutted road, she was sweating on what kind of reception awaited her.

They arrived at about the time the team had called it a day yesterday, and the empty car was still parked on the waterfront. As they skidded to a halt beside it Pete looked up towards the white walls of the villa and asked, 'Do you want to go up?'

'Hold on. Somebody's got to be still down here.' If diving was going on as usual that had to be a good sign. And a couple of students she had met yesterday came hurrying over, smiling, thank heaven, and actually apologising for their over-eager colleague. Everybody knew she must have been joking but, 'Halut,' one said scornfully, 'would not know a joke if it hit him.'

'I hope the next one does,' said Anni, and laughed with relief because they were smiling.

When the dinghy left the launch, chugging towards them, she strained to see who was aboard, and when she was spotted and somebody waved that had to be another good sign. She waved vigorously back and beside her Pete asked, 'Looking for Torba?'

'Yes.' She couldn't see Max. It was hard to distinguish everyone, but she was sure he was not there.

'See you tomorrow,' said Pete. He was not hanging around if there was going to be trouble, and she heard the roar of his motorbike as she went down on to the shingle to wait for them to climb out and wade ashore.

There was no Max. There was Jenny, Jimmy, Philippe and Henry, and, from their expressions, they were no longer hating her. 'Please, what's been happening?' she asked apprehensively.

'It's OK, I guess,' Jimmy told her. 'Max and Yusef were in police headquarters most of the day, but they seem to have convinced 'em in the end that it was all a mistake.'

'I am *sorry*,' said Anni. 'Me and my big mouth.'

Henry was quite jovial now, asking her, 'Had a good day? Ready to face the music? Max is not best pleased with you—he won't be suing you but he's seriously considering strangling you.'

'Well, if you've got to go you've got to go,' Anni said lightly, and she was still congratulating herself on coming through almost unscathed when she walked into the villa. But when Jimmy came downstairs and said, 'He wants to see you now,' her heart sank again. She had been an appalling nuisance and there was every chance that Max would tell her she had outstayed her welcome.

'It would be wise not to keep him waiting,' Philippe warned her grimly, and he was not teasing.

The study was two doors along from her bedroom, and she stood outside trying to prepare herself for the onslaught. It would be a quiet showdown—she couldn't imagine him losing his temper—while he flayed her with words that cut like a whip, and she was not sure she could take it. When she knocked on the door her hand seemed to have no strength in it.

He called, 'Come in,' and she stood in the doorway, looking across to where he was sitting at a desk by the open window. Even sitting down he seemed taller than she was. "Come in,' he said again, this time impatiently. 'And sit down,' and her feet dragged as she made for the nearest chair.

She said, 'What can I say? I've said enough, haven't I?'

'More than enough,' he agreed with her there. 'I'd be interested to know where you got your opinion of me.'

She repeated miserably, 'I was talking nonsense.'

'With your very good friend.'

Pete? There was a friend you could never rely on, a lightweight in every way, but she nodded. 'And I said I thought you would take what you wanted.' It was such a silly thing to cause so much trouble and she put a hand over her face, head down, because she could have wept at her own stupidity.

'Well, that's not too far off the mark,' he said drily, and as she looked up again, 'But I am not shipping out the city finds.'

'Of *course* not. Was it—awful today?'

'It was stimulating.' She bet it was. 'Luckily it ended in handshakes all round.'

It seemed like the best news she had had in years, because he didn't seem to be blaming her any more. She asked, 'You don't want me to sign anything, do you?'

'I don't want you to do a thing. If I could I'd lock you up until you had a plane booked for home.'

That could be telling her to get on a plane and go, but she was sure he was almost smiling and she said ruefully, 'Henry said you were ready to strangle me.'

'That had occurred to me.' This time his lips twitched and she risked a smile herself.

'If you locked me up I suppose I could pound the walnuts.'

'Not for me, you couldn't. Heaven knows what you'd be putting into the sauce. You'd be less likely to whet the sultan's appetite than knock the sultan out. They've had five untroubled years here, and within hours of your touching down we've got the *jandarma* overrunning us and me in police headquarters being frisked for marble statues.'

'They never,' she gasped.

'Damn near. It was one hell of a performance.'

She could imagine and she thanked her lucky stars that his sense of humour was keener than his sense of personal dignity. Well, it had finished with handshakes, and he had come out of it no whit diminished in anyone's eyes, she was sure of that, and she thought, If you were on my side I could take on the world.

She said, 'I had a grim day. I kept wondering what was happening here, and I deserved everything you said about me to Yusef this morning.'

'You understood?'

She grimaced, retorting, 'I didn't have to speak the language to follow that,' and when he laughed she joined in. Still smiling, he got up and came towards her, and she stood with a hand on the back of her chair for support because she was suddenly unsteady. For a moment she thought he was going to draw her to him, and when he didn't the disappointment was like a sharp pain, although she should not have expected anything of the sort.

She could stay and he didn't dislike her, but he had no overwhelming urge to get close to her, and if she had taken the first step and thrown her arms around him he would have detached her, still smiling.

She let go of the chair and followed him to the door. 'Go down and tell them you've taken a vow of silence,' he said, and she raised a hand like someone taking an oath.

'So help me, my lips are sealed,' she intoned. Her lips were dry and she looked at his mouth and longed to feel it against her own lips, crushing the breath out of her. The realisation of how much she wanted him scared her witless because he did not want her. Not like this.

As she walked away she heard the door close and she went into her own room. She couldn't go straight downstairs to rejoin the others. She couldn't face anybody just yet. Nothing in her life up to now had prepared her for needing a man so badly that she was aching for him, but she still had the sense to know that she must hide her feelings. Nobody must guess that she had developed a raging crush on Max.

She would not be the first nor the last, and, though they would probably treat her infatuation with kindly tolerance, she would embarrass them all. She would embarrass herself. And him. It was like a fever in her blood, and she would need all her health and strength to cool it.

Downstairs most of them were in the main room when she walked down the staircase. She smiled and so they knew that all was well and Jenny asked, 'Went all right, did it?'

'Well, he didn't kill me,' said Anni. She didn't

say, 'He didn't kiss me either. If he had done I might not have come down here again tonight.'

Next morning Anni's first waking thought was Max. As she lay there, warm and drowsy, she was permeated with longing and excitement as if she was just stirring from a sensuous dream. Which she knew she was, although she could hardly remember it.

Usually she was wide awake in seconds, but this morning she tried to hold on to the dream, so that she moved slowly and heavy-lidded through bathing and dressing. And when she was ready to go down and join them all the girl in the mirror with the secret smile looked like a stranger.

Her life had been changed. After Robert she had always held back, remembering the pain of rejection. That could come again. Max might want nothing from her. But other men did and he was the first she herself had wanted desperately.

She was finding him so different from the monster in her mind. She was finding how much she liked him, admired and respected him. Sexually he was overwhelmingly attractive and she fancied him so much that she wouldn't stop to count the cost if he ever came round to fancying her. She could wait for that. She would have to wait. For now just being near him, with his friends in his house, would have to be enough.

Although at first sight of him downstairs she had to check herself as she walked across the veranda, and shove her hands into her pockets because she wanted to touch him. On any excuse.

But any touch would be electric to her. She would either go scarlet or white, showing them all how she was feeling, and nobody must guess. Her reserve was deep, she could hardly handle this new vulnerability even as a secret, so she stayed a little distance from Max and talked brightly with Jenny.

For the rest of the week Max stayed in the villa, working on the last stages of a book about one of the trouble-spots of the world. Obviously he wanted nobody's company and Anni left with the team every morning. Down on the waterfront Pete and his motorbike were always waiting for her to take her sightseeing, and Pete was a cheerful fellow tourist.

He was also a resting actor, short of cash, and she usually paid for the meals over his token protests. She didn't mind. She was not being conned. Prices were cheap and she would have done the same with any companion who was broke. Pete was an amiable character, although most of his chatter drifted over her as she dreamed her dreams in which the man who sat beside her, walked and talked with her, was Max.

Her days started when she got back to the villa and Max joined them. He joined them all of course, all his guests, but she could pretend that sometimes he felt as she did when the rest faded away so that there was nobody but Anni and Max. Then his eyes seemed to speak to her as she was silently calling his name, until the rest of them rushed in on her again.

None of the wonders she saw with Pete stirred her like the deep timbre of Max's voice and the power of his physical presence. Nothing was as thrilling as wondering what Max could teach her, show her, down what wild and wonderful ways he might take her.

Each afternoon she was waiting on the waterfront for the team to go back to the villa, and she always said a firm goodbye to Pete then. She had no idea where he spent his nights, it was none of her business, and if one morning he had not been waiting she would hardly have missed him. She would have caught a bus or gone out to the launch, although she was saving the launch until the next time Max came down. That was where it had started for her, in the city under the sea. If she went diving with Max again this time could be the real beginning.

But before that happened that weekend a cruiser which looked like a small liner anchored in the bay with friends of Max on board. He was giving a party for them, and that was how Pete finally wangled another invitation to the villa, from Jimmy this time.

The villa was a superb setting for a party, the gardens lit with Chinese lanterns, music playing and buffet tables running the whole length of the white salon. And it seemed as if everybody who had been invited had managed to drive up the track, going by the number of guests pouring in.

The cruiser family had a stockbroker father, a mother who looked spectacular in oriental jewellery and a green and gold tunic trouser suit. And two knock-out daughters, a redhead and a blonde. They were the first arrivals, greeting or being introduced to the others as they arrived, the girls clinging to Max like limpets.

'They've adored Max ever since they were babies,' their mother said fondly, and Anni thought they sounded like screaming groupies. As it happened when she talked to them she found they were likeable girls, and it was a very good party.

Pete, with his showbiz looks and charm, was having a high old time. When Anni saw him he always seemed to have another plate of food and another drink, and was usually chatting up another of the rich-set guests.

She chatted and danced and enjoyed herself, getting compliments and admiring looks and more than a few invitations. The music was singing inside her when she went over to Max. She had more or less been watching him all evening long. He was always easy to spot, but this was the first time he had been alone in the crowd.

He stood in the shadows in the garden, and for once there was no one hanging on to him or talking to him, although any moment there would be, and when she reached him she said, 'Are you dancin'?' When he didn't answer at once, she added, 'Don't you know how it goes? You're supposed to say "Are you askin'?"'

'I have heard it.' He smiled down at her and his skin looked even darker against the white jacket and shirt. 'Are you asking?'

'Yes,' she said. 'Oh, yes.' She went into his

arms and she couldn't remember stumbling as she danced before. But after that first halting step it was everything she had known it would be. In the circle of his arms she was lost. Her cheek rested on his shoulder. With most men she could dance cheek to cheek, but he had to bow his head and she thought his lips brushed her hair and she felt her heart stop with delight. And then the closeness and the movement and the music were pure joy so that she looked up at him smiling and said, 'You dance well.'

'I don't,' he said. 'But you lie beautifully. And you dance beautifully too.'

She was a natural dancer, with an inborn sense of rhythm. She had never danced naked on the grass, but sometimes when she danced it seemed there was a wildness in her clamouring to get out. Usually she was happier at a distance, moving to the beat of the music, touching hands with her partner, but with Max she wanted to stay held by him, looking up at him. She could have danced forever in his arms.

'You have a lot of friends,' she said.

Even the gardens were crowded, and his smile was crooked as she asked, 'Don't you like having them around?'

'I wouldn't call all these friends. Acquaintances, most of them.'

Acquaintances who bored him, and she heard herself say, 'You can't, you know.'

'Can't what?'

'Clear off. Head for the hills.'

He looked at her as he had done when she'd

told him, 'I saw the tall towers,' then he said, 'You are an extraordinary girl. This is the first time tonight I haven't wanted to head for the hills.' They were laughing together and she thought the music must go on forever, because when it stopped the spell might be broken and this was the happiest she had ever been.

When it stopped a man plucked at Max's sleeve and there was a flurry of folk around him, but he still held Anni. Then he stroked her cheek and said, 'Don't run away.'

She could have said, 'I'll never run away again.' 'I'll be here,' she said.

After that she stopped dancing and went inside where there were all manner of people to talk to, and Max always had someone talking to him. Most of the guests left together, cars streaming out of the iron-scrolled gates and snaking in slow procession down the mountainside. If one seized up on the narrower bends there could be trouble, although these well-heeled party-goers looked as if transport never failed them.

The guests of honour were staying overnight, and when the last car had drawn away and the main door was closed Anni saw Pete. She hadn't seen him for ages, but now he was sitting on a settee in an alcove with the redhead from the cruiser and they looked engrossed in each other.

Pete was a guest because of Anni, but he was in no way her responsibility and she pretended she hadn't noticed him. She went upstairs with Jenny, both of them suddenly realising how late it was and how tired they were, and reached her own room where her bed looked so inviting that she could have flopped down fully dressed and gone to sleep.

When she was in bed, make-up stripped and lying between the cool sheets, she thought of Pete again. He was here for the night it seemed, but not for tomorrow night—she would see to that. She wondered if he was angling for a trip on the cruiser. Very likely, she thought. The scrounger afloat. Then she thought of nothing and nobody but Max, and stretched and relaxed and slept.

A knocking on her door woke her, so sharp and urgent that she was out of bed and stumbling to answer it still half asleep. She did grab a robe and, clutching it to her, opened the door, blinking into the dimly lit passage.

Pete stood there and she stared slack-faced with surprise while he looked fearfully back down the corridor and whispered hoarsely, 'For Pete's sake let me in.'

'What do you think you're doing?'

He was past her, into the room, and she was hopping mad. He had got himself into some sort of trouble and she wanted no part of it. 'The last I saw of you you were spinning Sandy the tale. What have you been trying on?' she demanded as she switched on the light.

He was wearing pyjamas and a dressing-gown that he had probably borrowed because there had been no prior overnight invitation. He was supposed to be getting a lift back to Idessa. Now he looked scared half to death as he sat down heavily. 'I've just bumped into Torba.'

'So what are you doing roaming around? Looking for Sandy's room? Looking for a bathroom?'

When he said, 'I was coming here, of course,' she was speechless. She had believed he'd accepted that there was no hope of a sexual fling with her. She had stressed that from the start, and yet he had taken the opportunity during the open-house of the party to track down her room, and he had the gall to imagine that if he presented himself at the dead of night all resistance would crumble. Either that or he was stoned out of his mind.

She said, 'You're a pain, do you know that? Get back to your own room.'

'All right,' he said, 'all right, but you can't blame me for trying. I thought the party spirit might still be in the air.'

'Not three hours after the party finished. Nor any other time. Out.'

She had a hand on the doorknob when he begged, 'Five minutes, *please*. I don't want to run into Torba again.'

'I don't care if you run into a sabre-toothed tiger, I want you out of my room.'

Pete raised a haggard face and said shakily, 'I was out of order, I'm sorry, but he scares the daylights out of me.'

'What are you talking about?'

'Well, I'm coming along the corridor, counting the doors, when suddenly he looms up.'

His study was just down the corridor; he worked all night sometimes.

'"Can I help you?" he says, and I don't know

what it is about him but I started sweating just looking at him. I said I knew where I was going, and he said that's always as well, and so help me I nearly started running. I'm still shaking, look at me.' He held out two hands showing a distinct tremor. 'You wouldn't have a drop of brandy in here?'

'I could find you an Alka Seltzer but that's as far as it goes,' Anni said heartlessly. 'Five minutes, then. Stay where you are, and after this you and I have come to the parting of the ways.'

'Anni——' he began.

'Don't say a word,' she said wearily, 'and don't move except in the direction of that door or I shall start screaming blue murder.'

She got back into bed, but she could hardly sleep with Pete slumped on the sofa. She could have shoved him out of the room but she didn't want raised voices that might disturb anyone else, so she gave him what she considered long enough to pull himself together. Then she sat up in bed and hissed, 'That's it. Goodnight.'

'All right, I'm going. You didn't mean it, did you—that you don't want to see me again?'

'It's been nice knowing you,' said Anni. 'But I cannot be doing with this.'

'Yeah,' said Pete, 'and I can tell you why in two words. Max Torba! You can't be doing with me because you'd rather be doing with him.'

'You do have a busy little mind.'

'I've got a mind that can add up and I've got eyes and ears too,' Pete sneered. 'You're here because of Torba, not because you can't afford a hotel.' His voice was getting shriller. 'But don't get your hopes up, chicken, because I haven't seen Max Torba chasing you. If he did he'd soon catch you, but you wouldn't hold him more than a week. Guys like him have birds like you dropping out of the trees.'

Then he looked out into the passage and, finding it clear, ran like a rabbit, leaving the door open. Anni got out of bed to close it, which she did quietly, locking it again and then sitting up in bed, her hands looped round her ankles.

Pete's spite had just bubbled up with a vengeance, but he was right. She was hooked on Max, well and truly caught. She would rather be in gaol with him than dining at the Ritz with any other man. And Pete could be right again. Max's interest in her might not last, but tonight when they danced he had enjoyed having her in his arms, and when he stroked her cheek and said, 'Don't run away,' that had been a caress.

In the morning she would say, 'I'm still here, I didn't run,' but tonight he had met Pete on his way to Anni's room, and what would he make of that? Surely he'd know she hadn't been expecting Pete—although how would he know?

She was out of bed, halfway to the dooor, when she stopped herself because she could hardly go looking for Max at this time of night. Better wait till morning. Then she would tell him just what the relationship was between herself and Pete, and when she had done that she would tell him other things that she had never told a living soul.

He still remembered that New Year's Eve party

when he had thought she was a spoilt teenager, hurting for the fun of it. His opinion of her had been based on that, even if he did seem to be changing his mind. Tomorrow she would talk to Max and Max would listen, and as for Pete's gibe about birds like her falling out of trees—so what, so long as Max caught her?

CHAPTER FIVE

ANNI slept peacefully and woke feeling good, as if she had already talked to Max. But while she was dressing she began to have doubts. She could explain about Pete; she was sure he would believe her there. It was the thought of raking up the past that worried her. That could hurt like ripping open an old wound where poison still festered, while he might consider the whole thing childish and silly. He might even laugh. If he did she would laugh too, and be sick later because she was feeling sick now just remembering how it was.

It was so quiet when she came out of the corridor to the top of the stairs that she was wondering if she was first up, although she had slept late, but then she saw several of the team down below. They were sitting quietly, hardly talking at all. The party had taken its toll and as Anni joined them Henry yawned and said, 'If you're looking for your boyfriend he's still chatting up the girls.'

'Good,' said Anni crisply. 'Maybe he'll hitch a lift to Australia. Is Max around?'

'Somewhere,' said Jimmy. 'I saw him not long ago.'

She went towards the terrace where most of the

others were gathered, including Pete, who deliberately turned his back on her. After last night no wonder he couldn't look her in the face. But Max was not there and she walked around, looking into ground-floor rooms, knocking on his study door, and at last going out into the gardens.

She saw him then, well away from the house, walking alone with nobody near, and she felt a flutter of panic as she made herself walk towards him. He turned and waited and she said, 'You told me not to run away.'

'So I did.'

'About Pete.'

'Ah, yes,' he drawled. 'He found your room?'

She knew he had seen Pete knock on her door and she said, 'He did. And gave me the shock of my life because I didn't think he'd be staying the night here, much less arriving outside my bedroom.' She felt he relaxed although his face told her nothing and she went on, 'You scared him out of his wits, and he isn't that bright to begin with or he wouldn't have been looking me up in the early hours.'

Now he smiled. 'He did look shifty, but I can't recall posing any threat.'

'You're a lot bigger than he is,' she said gaily, 'and you caught him creeping around. He was asking for brandy—which I didn't have—and five minutes' start in case he bumped into you again, before I threw him out.'

'You are joking.'

'That is the truth, every word. You scared him and I was a big disappointment.'

'Between us we seem to have been hard on the poor chap. Should I apologise?' That was a laugh, but she pretended he was serious, looking up at him with dancing eyes.

'What for? It's not your fault that you gave him the shakes and I can't see what I did to be sorry for.'

'You might have offered him a drink.'

'I don't keep a bottle of brandy with me, and anyhow I wanted him running scared not tanked up with Dutch courage.'

He burst out laughing and so did she. 'There was something else,' she said, and bit her lip because everything was fine. She should cast no shadow on this and she wished she could have called back her words.

'What?'

'Nothing.'

They were standing by a giant magnolia tree, laden with waxy greenish white blossoms, and she remembered the mulberry tree. How he had walked round it when she was laughing at Robert. Max was kind but he was also a cynical man of the world. Her teenage trauma would hardly rate as a tragedy with him and she wished she hadn't started this.

But he was waiting and she said, 'It doesn't matter.' She gave a small shrug to show what a small matter it was, and he put his hands on her shoulders so that the shrug turned into a shiver right to the end of her toes.

'Tell me.' Men had looked into her eyes before and thought they could read her thoughts. None of them had, but she felt that he might, and she closed her eyes briefly, her long lashes lying on her flushed cheeks, then she looked up at him and knew that whatever he did he would not laugh at her. But she had to move away a little and she had to turn her face away.

She said, 'I—I want to explain something. That New Year's Eve party when you heard me talking and you said I was a brat pack all on my own. You remember that, I know you do, and I wanted to tell you what you don't know.'

She had folded her arms so that they were wrapped tight around her and she stared at a blossom as though she were trying to memorise it. 'When I was seventeen,' she said, 'I was plain and fat.' She'd been starved of affection; comfort eating had made her overweight. 'So that when the first man to pay me any attention at all said he loved me I lost my head. He didn't love me, of course, but he played me along, as a joke I suppose.

'Anyhow, one day when I was at home alone— well, I knew I was ugly but I thought that wasn't how Robert saw me, until I was naked and— repulsive, I suppose, and he laughed at me and said, "You're not very good at kissing, you know, not much of a turn-on at all. Ever thought of losing some weight? Underneath all this flab there could be quite a sexy little body. Not smart, but you might be sexy. Get dressed, sweetie, you're beginning to bore me."'

It sounded what it was, a young man's callous cruelty, but it had destroyed every illusion of a sensitive girl who had come close that night to destroying herself. 'That stopped me overeating,' she said. She had been unable to face food for weeks. 'After that the weight dropped off and at that party I felt fantastic.

'I hadn't seen Robert in a long time, and when he began to follow me around I let him. And out in the garden, well, you heard me getting my own back. It wasn't very nice—I suppose in a way I should have been thanking him. Anyhow, I said to him more or less what he'd said to me, and he cleared off and you walked round the tree, but I never said anything like that to anyone else—I never was a one-girl brat pack.'

He said gently, 'And you never were ugly, not with those eyes.' She turned to face him then and he added, 'As many a man since must have told you.'

'Well, yes.' She thought they made her look like a hungry cat, but she had never been short of admirers who waxed lyrical about her slanting smoky grey eyes that looked as if they would glow in the dark.

'You never married?' he asked her.

'No. Nor you?' She knew he hadn't, she would have read about that because he was news, but she could have married and parted in the past eight years with hardly anyone knowing or caring.

He said, 'I always seem to be on the move. And it's not a state for which I feel particularly suited.'

'Me neither.' She sounded carefree, and the choice had been hers, but she was not letting him know why her relationships had ended. Where she had stopped and drawn back. It would make her sound gauche and awkward and she was not. She was a woman who could get almost any man she wanted, but who had never wanted any of them deeply and intimately, until she came here and found him.

'What are your plans for today?' he asked her.

'I haven't any.'

That wasn't true. Her plan was to be with him, and when he said, 'Shall we head for the hills?' she replied,

'I would like that very much; I'll get a hat.'

'I'll wait for you.'

She thought those were the loveliest words she had ever heard, and she ran back to the house and her room with wings on her feet. The day was already humid, she should have been going slowly, but she grabbed her hat and bag, desperate to get back to him, and carried on running until she saw him again. He was still where she had left him and she slowed down then, but smiled all the way until she was near enough to touch.

She didn't touch and neither did he, but he smiled at her. 'Are they still there?'

'I think so.' She had passed folk in the villa but she could hardly have said now who they were. They had all seemed shadowy, as though it was only out here that everything was sharp and brilliant.

'Then we'll go this way.'

There was a gate in the wall, and through it they came out on the mountainside behind the villa. As the gate clanged behind them she asked, 'Where are we going?'

'Just escaping.'

'Best offer I've had all day.'

He leered at her. 'The day's young yet.'

'Promises, promises,' she chanted.

They climbed slowly in the blistering heat, taking the shade of a cypress tree or an overhanging shelf of rock. Below lay the villa. On the lower slopes were the olive groves and patches of cultivated land, below them the sea.

Over on the coastline towards the right lay the ruins of an amphitheatre. Broken semicircles of stone seating showed where the crowds had gathered for spectacles that could end in a bloodbath, when the city under the sea stood on dry ground. Now sightseers swarmed like ants and Max said, 'You must see it by moonlight when the tourists have gone.'

'Oh, I must,' she said.

Mostly they walked without talking, but the silence seemed more meaningful to her than never-ending chatter with another man. She knew that he was aware of her all the time, and without touching or talking he was reaching her. Every time he looked at her she felt happiness soaking into her like the sun and glowing deep inside her.

But the climb was hard going. She was beginning to flag a little when he led the way up a particularly steep rise, through scrub grass and stunted trees, and she asked, 'Do we have to? Couldn't we go at it gradually?'

'You wouldn't want to miss this,' he said.

'Want to bet?' She took his outstretched hand and he pulled her up, and as she struggled along she gasped, 'Where did you get your training, up the Matterhorn?'

'Funny you should say that,' he said.

There was a slight flattening in the ground here where one hardy tree grew, and a fall of overhanging bushes and creepers which he pulled aside. 'A cave?' She gave a cry of delight, peering past the tree into the shadowy dark. 'Shade!'

Caves were cool, even on a mountainside, and as he held back the curtain of foliage she could see that this was large enough to walk around in. 'Better than shade,' he said.

With the entrance opened there was still sunlight when they were both inside and she could hear what sounded like running water. She dropped her hat and bag and asked incredulously, 'Is that a freak echo? It can't be a babbling brook.'

'Near enough,' he said, and from a tiny fissure right at the back of the cave a little spring bubbled, filling a hollow in the rocky earth the size of a man's cupped hands and then vanishing. An underground stream from the mountain-top.

She knelt down on the shingle. The water was cold on her lips when she drank from the basin, and the spring splashed her face so that she looked up smiling and blinking. 'That was out of this world.'

He knelt down beside her, scooping up water, telling her, 'If I'd known you were coming I'd have brought a bottle of wine to cool.'

'Do you do that? Come up here?' What she really meant was, who shares your wine?

'Yes. Sometimes to read. Sometimes to write. I have slept up here.'

Alone? she wondered, and asked, 'Does it get cold at night?'

'Not if you come prepared.'

'With blankets? Or the right company?'

'Preferably both.'

He was smiling, but jealousy knifed her at the thought of him lying in the shadows with some other woman, and she had to dabble her fingertips in the little basin, playing for a moment of time to get the right note of gaiety in her voice when she said, 'If only they'd asked our readers to name the man they'd choose to be stuck up a mountainside with you'd have got my vote.'

'I'm delighted to hear it.' He was sprawled back now, arms behind his head, using the rocky wall of the cave as backrest. 'What are you on about?'

'Last year the magazine I work for ran a popularity poll to find the man you'd enjoy being marooned with on a desert island, and you came top.'

He grinned. 'That was your lot, was it? I remember that. They sent me three dozen red roses and a bloody great card, "The readers of *Go-Girl* have voted you their desert-island dish".'

It had all been a giggle and she was giggling now. 'You sent us a very nice letter back saying how flattered you were.'

'Flattered? I was flabbergasted. They must all have been out of their minds.'

She pretended to be giving a serious explanation. 'They needed a boat builder. Or failing that somebody to knock up a hut and bring home the dinner—you could have done that for them, couldn't you?'

'Marooned with your readers I'd probably concentrate on the boat.'

She fell back in mock horror. 'They *would* be disappointed, because what they really wanted was to be kept warm at night. They all seemed to have this idea that you would keep their fires stoked up.'

Her double meaning was mischievously clear and he said, 'As well as build a house and catch the food and maybe build a boat? They're a greedy bunch, your readers.'

'No, they're not, they're a lovely bunch. What did you do with the roses?' She supposed they had been sent to his London address and she wondered what that was like. She couldn't imagine him in a bower of blooms—a garden was another matter.

'Spread them around,' he said. 'Half a dozen here, half a dozen there.'

'You gave them away?' She imagined long-legged lovelies with long-stemmed roses and hoped the roses had had thorns.

'I'm afraid so.'

'Well, it's nice to know we made your ladies happy.'

'It was very generous of you. They appreciated it. I gather I didn't get your vote.'

'Staff couldn't vote, but you did all right with all

the rest. They all agreed with the verdict.' She looked at the bright greenery in the mouth of the cave. 'I was the odd woman out because I said——'

She paused and waited and of course he asked, 'You said what?'

'I said I'd rather be cast away with a gorilla.'

She was grinning and it was incredible that she should be telling him this and that he should be saying, 'Good lord, woman, how hairy do you want 'em? What's wrong with that?'

He flexed brown, muscular arms, and bared a hairy chest, and she said, 'Not a thing. You make a smashing gorilla, and, as my editor said, where would you find a gorilla with a sexy voice?'

He did a send-up of a sexy drawl. 'That's smart thinking.'

'She's a smart girl. Do you want to meet her?'

'No.'

'Good, because she looks like Kate O'Mara and I've always been jealous of her.'

'No, you haven't,' he said, and he was right. She had never really been jealous of anyone, except the women in his life, and right now not even of them.

'Tell me about your readers,' he said.

'Why?'

'Because I want to know about them. I know hardly anything about you.'

She sat with his arm around her on the shingle floor of the cave, with the green light filtering in and the murmuring music of the little spring, bathed in a comforting security that she had never known before. It was not just a sensual reaction. That too, of course, but it was as though she had found the friend she had been looking for for a long time.

She began to tell him about her readers, bright women because she worked for a go-ahead magazine that covered a wide range of interests, with a touch of nonsense occasionally, like the desert-island quiz which was timed for a holiday edition.

She described her colleagues and her home, some of the stories she had covered, some of the things she had done since she got her first job as a trainee reporter. When she paused he made her go on and she talked freely, but only about life since her father sold their home. Before that was another life and another girl. She was Anni not Annabel now, and the future was golden.

She drank from the spring again and he asked her, 'Do you have any family?'

'There was just Roger and me. And my father, of course. My mother died when I was born.' Her father had never forgiven her for that. After Roger was killed he said, 'Why are you always the one left alive? Why couldn't it have been you?' and he had hardly spoken to her again.

She asked, 'Do you have a family?'

'No. My father reared me. He was a war correspondent. It got too much for my mother, she left him for a Texas multimillionaire, and I was in boarding-schools until I went to university. Then one afternoon he rode a motorbike up a track in Cambodia and disappeared.'

There would be no hope after nearly twenty

years but his son must have prayed that the end
was quick, and she said, 'I'm sorry.'

'So was I, although we were almost strangers.'

It seemed they had never been strangers, she
and Max. There had been such loneliness in her
that finding a man with so much strength and
tenderness was a little miracle, bringing her to life
where her heart had been closed and cold. Her
spirit was opening like a flower as her body would
blossom when he made love to her.

They talked about all manner of things—laughing at each other's jokes, easy in each other's
company—long enough for the fierce heat of the
day to subside. 'We'll go back to the villa,' he said.
'Get the car and drive out somewhere.'

'Get the others, you mean?'

'Certainly not.' Her spirits soared again and she
dipped her hands once more in the little basin of
the spring, touching her lips and temples with
coolness.

He was holding the fall of creepers aside for her
to duck under and as she straightened in the open
air he seized her, his hands around her waist
lifting her high. When he put her down again her
dazzled eyes followed his gaze to where a thin
black snake slithered into the undergrowth.

She gulped and croaked, 'Did I nearly tread on
that?' Of course she had. 'Is it poisonous?'

'Only if it's attacked.'

'Would it know I wasn't attacking it?'

Which was a daft question, and he smiled as he
said, 'Now that I can't vouch for.'

'Well, thank you.'

'My pleasure.'

'Mine too,' she said, and she took his hand and, as they came together down the mountainside, she felt that his touch was all the support she would ever need.

They walked round the villa to where the cars were garaged. There had to be folk in the villa, gardeners in the grounds, but they met no one and drove away from a house that seemed to be sleeping in the afternoon sun.

They stopped for a meal in a little town, sitting on a terrace overlooking the gardens of a Greek Orthodox church, eating succulent prawns and spiced wild rice. Anni thought it was the most delicious food she had ever tasted. Just as the wine was sharper and sweeter than any wine she could remember.

'I'm having a wonderful day,' she said.

'So am I,' Max agreed.

All week Pete had been a stand-in while her thoughts were on Max, but now Max was with her. The real man was not a daydream. And meeting his eyes made everything seem dangerous and exciting.

She thought, I love the way you look. The slow way you smile. Sometimes a grin that would make anyone smile back. Sometimes just a twitch of the lips, and best of all when you smile with your eyes from under the heavy lids. I love your big beautiful body with the taut, hard muscles and the co-ordination of a tiger, your thick dark hair, your strong mouth and your strong hands.

I could sit here for hours and watch your mouth

and your hands. I can feel them touching me just watching them. And I like the way you sound. I could listen to your voice for the rest of my life. . .

Lights were on in the villa when they drove through the open gates, and the team had just finished their evening meal. When the overnight guests were leaving this morning there had been a search for Max, and later for Anni. They were surprised to find them both missing, but only Jenny was really intrigued. She had seen Pete, making up to the girls and driving away with the cruiser family, and felt sorry for Anni. She hoped that Max had taken her somewhere to cheer her up, and when they walked in together she saw that the cheering up had worked because Anni was radiant.

The days in the sun had tanned her skin to dark honey and whitened the blonde streaks in her mid-brown hair, but it was more than that. Today's heat should have drained her, but she looked vividly alive, and for the first time Jenny realised that she was not just beautiful but breathtaking.

In the week that followed Anni woke each morning hardly able to believe her luck. She couldn't get downstairs fast enough and it was all because of Max. He was a life enhancer. When she was with him everything was magical. She made friends with local farmers and fishermen, shopkeepers, restaurant owners, because they were Max's friends; by the end of the week she had picked up enough of the language to follow some of the talk without him having to translate for her.

When he praised her, 'You've got a good ear for languages,' she grinned.

'The other one's not bad either,' she retorted, and he took her into a little shop, in a narrow whitewashed street, and bought her a pair of gold earrings.

She had hoped they were for her when the salesgirl brought them out of the window and Max asked her, 'Do you like them?'

'They're gorgeous,' she had declared. But when he handed them to her she said, 'For me?'

'Who else?' She didn't know their names, and these days she never thought about other women who would be delighted to be getting earrings or anything else from him.

This week she had no rivals and she took out the turquoise studs she had been wearing and fumbled with the thin golden wire, pushing it in place, moving her head so that the earring swung against her cheek with a tinkle of tiny bells.

Max held the other earring and she lifted her hair and turned to him, and closed her eyes, smiling, because she always felt swoony when he touched her. One of these days she was going to melt right into him, but this afternoon she stayed upright while he slipped in the earring and said, 'You're not just a pair of pretty ears.'

'Oh, I'm pretty all over,' she said gaily.

'That you are,' he told her, as if they were lovers, and the salesgirl watched wistfully as they walked out into the sunshine.

It seemed to Anni that there was a growing intimacy between them going back for years. A total turn-around from the old resentment. He had not made physical love to her, but every day in every other way he took possession of her, and she loved it.

Something extraordinary was always happening. Later that day they were in an isolated village when the procession went by. Villagers watched in silence while three tourists chattered and took photographs of the man at the head who was holding high a staff with the bronze effigy of a snake. 'Who are they?' Anni asked.

Max told her quietly, 'The peacock angels. A centuries-old cult of devil worshippers.'

'Is it a secret society?' Anni whispered. 'Don't they mind being photographed?'

'Oddly,' said Max, 'films rarely come out well. That chap's wasting his time.'

He wasn't joking, and she stood very close to him, touching an earring under the fall of her hair as if no evil could reach her while Max was with her.

Everywhere was fabulous. They went to Troy, which seemed to be all deep trenches and great mounds of earth and stones, but Max brought it to life for her. When he described the long seige she could imagine the soldiers camped below the walls of the city to which Helen, the most beautiful woman in the world and the runaway wife of a king, had fled with her lover. They'd had ten years together before the city went up in flames and Helen was dragged back home, and driving away Anni sighed for the lovers, and for the nameless ones who had died on the pyre of their passion.

'They had a lot to answer for, didn't they, Helen and Paris?'

'They certainly did,' Max agreed cheerfully. 'I always wondered what Menelaus said to her when he finally got her home.'

The mind boggled and Anni began to smile. 'Maybe that's what he said.' She dropped her voice to a masculine growl. '"What have you got to say for yourself?"'

'Well?' he demanded after a moment, turning a thunderous scowl on her playing Menelaus, so she was playing Helen now and she switched to a virago shrillness.

'Well, I hope you're satisfied. Your mates have made a right mess of Troy.'

'Sorry about that, pet,' he said sheepishly, and she collapsed in giggles, her head on his shoulders.

Moonlight silvered the ruins of the amphitheatre while the waters of the bay shimmered in the darkness when they reached Nidus. Max slowed down the car, pulling off the road, and Anni looked down at the sea. She was hot and grimy and the water would be cool. 'Could I go for a swim?' she asked.

'What in the world's to stop you?'

This late the whole coastline was deserted, she could have the sea all to herself, but she wanted him to share it. 'You too,' she said.

'Of course.'

The moon was bright on the path down to the little cove so that she hardly needed guiding, but she took Max's hand because it was good to reach for someone and know they would be there. These days she had grown so accustomed to having him with her that it was hard to believe in a time or place without him. Home, job, friends—none of it seemed real any more.

Little waves lapped the shore and a rock shelf led out into deeper water. Max walked to the edge of it and said, 'The swimming's good from here. I sometimes swim very early or very late.'

He stripped off his shirt, stepped out of his sandals and trousers as she pulled her dress over her hair, keeping her head bent, fumbling with a bra fastening. He was quite unselfconscious about his nakedness as he dived off the rock while she was still hunched and wriggling.

She had to strip, and why not? Her breasts were firm, her stomach was flat and her legs were long. This was sheer prudery, but she was overcome with sudden shyness and she dived into the water, frantic to cover up.

When she surfaced he was swimming alongside and the water foaming around her as she cleaved through it felt like caressing hands. When her kicking leg brushed him she almost expected him to wrap powerful arms around her and drag her down to the depths. If he had it would have been water games, no more, but she turned and swam away, going fast even when she knew he was not following her.

It was peaceful all alone, floating on the water

with the white moon and stars up there. Her heart had stopped thumping and she lay back, letting the gentle swell of the sea support her, sculling with outstretched hands.

Nobody caught her hand this time. Max was swimming a long way out. She saw the dark head moving in the dark water. He came down here, very early or very late, when there was no one else around, and swam alone, so this was how he liked it best. He was a loner by nature and that was very different from being lonely.

But she wished he had followed her. She wanted him with her and she wanted him to make love to her, although he had no idea that he would be the first man. The first even to see her naked since Robert had laughed at her.

He was swimming back now, so there was no chance of her getting out first and getting some clothes on, and she followed slowly, seeing him draw himself up on to the rocks. He was magnificent in the moonlight. His skin gleamed as if it had been oiled, and when he reached down an arm to help her get out he had almost to drag her up because she hadn't the strength to help herself.

Having got her out, he looked into her face with sharp concern. 'Are you all right?'

'Fine.' But she was gasping.

'Sit down.' She slithered down, her back to the rough rock of the cliff, as soon as he let her go, and he put his shirt round her shoulders, blaming himself. 'You are tired. It's been a long day.'

She was not tired. Her muscles had seized up because his nakedness and her own had almost paralysed her. She was knocked out, but that wasn't the sort of thing a woman who was supposed to be experienced could explain to a sophisticated man, and she began to dry herself, babbling, 'I was all right, the water's so warm, did you stop for the amphitheatre?'

'Yes.'

'Can we go?'

'It's the right time to see it. Are you up to it?' He was dressed in trousers, carrying his sandals. She was still using his shirt as a towel.

'Of course.' Her skin was damp and her clothes stuck to her, but she got into them quickly and didn't look at him again until she got up from easing on her blue canvas slip-ons over wet feet.

He picked up his wet shirt, and threw it over his left shoulder, taking her arm as they made their way across the rocks, over the shingle, and started to climb. And she wondered what kind of fool he would think her if he knew that the sight of him just now in the moonlight had made her feel as inexperienced and fearful as a Victorian virgin.

There had been some reconstruction to the amphitheatre, but hardly enough to count. Undergrowth had been cleared so that the rows of stepped seating were revealed as broken stones. The half-circle of the arena was bare hard earth, and, backing it, stumps of pillars were all that remained of buildings and terraces.

But this was where the citizens of the city had come on their high days, and Anni asked, 'Was it always gladiators and wild animals tearing each other to pieces?'

'Not always. They'd take a good play or music sometimes.'

'Oh, I'm glad, I'd have hated it to be nothing but horrors. Maybe there'll be dancing tonight.' She laughed, shaking her hair, still wet and tangled, and yelped in dismay, 'Oh, *no*, I've lost an earring!'

She dragged fingertips through her hair, frantically searching, frisking her clothing in case it was hooked somewhere. But it was not. It was probably in the sea; she should never have gone swimming in earrings that had no safety catch. She hadn't been thinking about the earrings, but she had been so careful with them until then. She had touched them again and again and loved the feel of them against her cheeks.

She beat clenched fists against the air as if it were a wall and howled, 'How could I *do* that?'

'It's no great matter,' Max soothed her. 'If we don't find it we'll get this one matched for you.'

'Can you? Would you do that?' A substitute would be the next best thing. It had seemed as if she had lost something irreplaceable and the relief was overwhelming. 'They're my treasure trove,' she said. 'I'm sure they're bringing me luck.'

'Are you fond of jewellery?'

'What woman isn't? I've always worn rather discreet stuff, stud earrings, the odd ring and gold chain, but maybe I'll go in for something bolder because I love these earrings.'

She made sure that the survivor was securely

through her ear, and he asked, 'Have you ever heard of the jewels of Helen?'

'Our Helen? Helen of Troy?'

'Yes, our Helen.' She shook her head. 'Well, when Troy was being excavated about a hundred years ago a hoard of jewellery was found which, the story went, belonged to Paris's father and could have been worn by Helen. The man who was footing the bill for the dig got them out of the country in his wife's luggage and she wore them at social gatherings in Athens. They were magnificent and Sophie was a sensation, before they had to be handed over. They ended in Berlin.'

'The jewels of Helen,' Anni said dreamily. 'She must have felt like the sexiest woman alive wearing them! They would be glittering, barbaric and beautiful. Even when she was old the memory of them must have made her feel young again. Are they in a museum?'

'They vanished after the war when the Russians went into Berlin, and their whereabouts have been a mystery ever since. But——' He smiled and she gasped.

'Do you know?'

'I've travelled some of the trail over the years. It started with some papers that my father left and it's been something of an undercover hobby. I keep my files here, only a few of my very closest friends know about it.'

She was thrilled that he was trusting her with a secret so few shared. 'You'll find them,' she said, 'I know you will.'

'It's a long way from sure, but if I do you shall wear them, for five minutes at least.'

He would keep his promise if he could, and she said, 'Then I'll be young forever. Tell me what they looked like.' She moved closer, smiling. 'Put them on me.'

'A gold filigree collar with stones of lapis lazuli,' he said and she lifted her hair for him to 'fasten' the clasp over the nape of her neck, and she knew how it would look. The jewelled collar, the pearls, and the chains that roped over her head. The ornate head-dress, the earrings, the wide bracelets covering her arms and a ring for every finger. His fingers rested lightly, brushing briefly, and from every contact she felt a tingling coursing through her veins.

When he stood back she could imagine the weight of the fabulous jewels and feel in her own body Helen's blazing beauty that had set an ancient world on fire. She stepped into the centre of the arena and turned, swaying to silent music. 'Did they dance here?' she asked. 'Shall I dance for you?'

He sat down, all her audience in a theatre designed for thousands, and she hummed a tune under her breath. No particular music, just something to sway and swirl to. She danced languorously at first, her hands crossing and undulating close to her body, but gradually the vast space around her loosened her gestures until she was moving as freely as she sometimes danced in her dreams. Never in real life.

She kicked off her shoes and danced with the

passion of a born seductress and the wildness of a woman just out of gaol. If Helen danced she would dance this way, Anni thought crazily, and she laughed across at the man she was dancing for.

When she had whirled herself to a standstill she threw her arms wide then let them fall, and waited for him to reach her, her head thrown back still laughing.

That had been fantastic. Her blood had been calling to Max as Helen's must have called to Paris. . .love me, love me, love me, nothing else matters, there is nothing else. . .

But that was over three thousand years ago, and now was now, and love me meant take me, here on the hard ground, and she was panicking again. When he reached her she had stopped laughing. He put hands on her upper arms and felt her flinch, and looked into her face as she stammered, 'No,' and then, 'Not here.'

All her fire ebbed away when he smiled at her and shook his head. Then he picked up her shoes and brought them to her and she shoved her dusty feet into them. 'Come on, baby, time to go home,' he said, as if she were a wild child who had stayed too long at the party.

CHAPTER SIX

MAX said goodnight to Anni at her bedroom door and went off to his room down another corridor. In the car she had pretended to be sleepy because that way she didn't have to talk. She had stumbled upstairs and at her door he had said, 'Goonight, sleep well,' and, smiling at her, had kissed her and left her.

She had wanted him to hug her and then she might have said, 'I'm sorry I panicked but you don't know how this is for me. This my first affair and you don't know how scared I am, but I do want you to want me.'

She might have to say something like that because soon he was going to realise that he was not dealing with a woman of sexual experience and tonight he had wanted her. While she was dancing and before she started shaking and screaming, but not enough to lose his own self-control. He was a man who took what he wanted, but he had not wanted her enough to take her, although if he had caressed her as a woman instead of treating her like an overtired child he could have pierced her defences and unleashed a flood of passion.

That was how it should have been and she lay back on the pillows, imagining a different ending to the dance where she went eagerly into his arms, and her dreams were sweet and sensuous and savage.

Until she woke when it was nearly morning and her final dream was a mini-nightmare. She was running through the burning streets of Troy, and she came out of that one sitting bolt upright in bed in a cold sweat of terror. She rocked herself awake and kicked off the sheets.

If Max had been sleeping beside her, as he would have been, as he should have been, he would have woken and she would have said, 'I've just been back to Troy. I was there for the last battle.'

He would say, 'You picked a hell of a time to drop in,' and gather her up beside him.

She would smile against the rise and fall of his chest and feel his laughter on her lips. The days weren't enough. She needed him through the nights and then there would be no nightmare that could frighten her.

But next morning, for the first morning in over a week, he had plans that did not include her. A mailbag full of letters and packages had been delivered and when he said he must deal with them she said quickly, 'Of course.'

'Come out with us,' said Henry, so that was her day arranged for her. But on the beach she changed her mind about joining them on the launch. Without Max she really would rather be without anybody. So she made an excuse for going into town.

'I should be phoning the office. I haven't been in touch since I left and this is supposed to be a working holiday. And I could always do some shopping. I'll be here at the usual time.'

But she had no intention of phoning anybody and no plans to go anywhere in particular. She just wanted to wander around on her own.

She caught a bus and then a taxi and wandered the streets of a little town, pretending again that Max was with her, talking to him in her mind. Hello there, Max, I think I love you, I know I do and I'm almost sure that you're going to love me.

For the first time she wondered if Max was a shortening of a longer name: Maxim? Maxwell? Surely not Maximilian? She laughed to herself and got answering smiles from hopefuls who thought she was smiling at them, and shook her head and walked on if they approached her.

Most of the time she was in a happy trance, so that later she could hardly have said where she went or what she saw. She window-shopped, strolling through markets. There was nothing she really needed to buy, although she would have liked to have found a gift to take back. A small thing to show that she had thought of him on a day when she had never stopped thinking of him, but what did you get the man who had everything?

In the end she picked up a small painted dish, garish in reds and greens and gold, because of the crimson rose at the centre of the design. She would say, 'You know I was the only one on the staff who was against sending you the red roses? Well, I've changed my mind. So here's my rose and you can choose the island.'

It would be a joke, but if he named an island she would say, 'It's a date.'

By mid-afternoon she was longing to go back. She could climb up to the villa and he might have finished with his mail—he might be missing her. But he needed time on his own and the last thing she wanted was for him to start thinking she was hanging around like a clinging vine. He had plenty of that from other women, so she made herself walk down another road instead of running back to him.

She was sitting on the sea wall near to where the car was parked, drowsy in the heat and waiting for the others, when Pete whispered, 'Hello, chicken,' in her ear and she nearly fell off the wall.

She turned to glare up at him and he spread his hands wide, looking contrite. 'Sorry, sorry, I shouldn't have said that about you and Max Torba. That was over the top.'

'No, it wasn't,' Anni snapped. 'It was right on target.'

'I reckoned it was,' Pete said ruefully. 'Getting on with him all right now, are we?'

'Yes, thank you. What are you doing here? Didn't you manage to cadge a berth with the Connollys?'

'As it happens I did. Over to Rhodes where they were picking up another couple. But that's not why I'm here, I came to tell you my news. I rang my agent yesterday and there's a very nice little opening in the offing.'

Anni's annoyance gave way, she was pleased

for him, and she said warmly, 'That's splendid. Acting? TV commercials?'

'A TV play that could make a series. I'm flying out tomorrow afternoon, but I had to come and tell you because I think you've been my good-luck girl.'

'I don't see how,' said Anni, 'but of course I wish me luck. Now, tell me about it.'

He sat down on the sea wall beside her. The story line seemed vague and not very original, a thriller about a jewel thief, and she hoped it would be a success. Showbiz was a risky business. Pete was good-looking but she hadn't seen any evidence of blinding charisma or burning ambition in him. Of course, she had never seen him acting; maybe he was on his way to fame and fortune.

'Give me an interview next time you're my way,' she said, 'and I shall boast that I knew you before you hit the big time.'

A shadow crossed his face, and perhaps she was making it sound too easy because he said, 'It might not work out. Nothing's a dead cert, is it?' and she had to agree.

'I suppose not.'

She would like to believe that Max felt the longing for her that she felt for him, but nothing was sure and Pete said shakily, 'You're even more stunning than I remember. Are you really hooked on Torba?'

'I am rather.'

'Is he down here?'

'I think he's in the villa.'

'You wouldn't take up with me?'

She tried not to laugh because it was such an impossible idea, telling him gravely, 'You'll travel faster alone, and I do wish you all the luck in the world.'

He threw his arms around her in one of those theatrical embraces that she had received countless times, and she heard Jenny's 'Hi' coming over the water from the dinghy that was sailing towards the shore. They must be looking like a very affectionate couple, clasped together, and Jenny for one would be wondering what on earth was happening.

Jenny was first out of the dinghy, splashing her way through the shallow water. She called 'Hello' before she reached them, and when she did she said, 'We didn't expect to see you again so soon.'

Pete gave her a flashing smile and Anni said, 'It's just a brief call. He's landed a part in a TV play and he thought we'd like to hear about it.'

'Congratulations,' said Jenny. 'Is it a big part?'

'Yes,' Pete said smugly.

'I suppose it's like us coming up with a goodie from the city.'

'That's right,' said Pete. 'I haven't had too many breaks up to now. Nothing that meant big money, but this could be it.' His eyes were gleaming and Anni suspected he would still be tight-fisted even if he did strike it rich, but it was none of her business and it was always pleasant to hear somebody's good news.

When the rest of the team reached them and Jenny said, 'Pete's just got a TV role,' they were not over-impressed. They were all sufficiently well-known to have made TV appearances, and Pete Hartley was an actor who usually seemed pleased with himself, so they expected him to be acting.

But they congratulated him and said it was nice to see him again, and Pete asked, 'Would it be all right if I joined you? I've got to be off first thing in the morning, but would he let me doss down, do you reckon?'

'He' was Max of course, and they were all looking at Anni as if Pete's presence might embarrass her. She shrugged because she didn't care what Pete did and Henry said, 'Well, there's plenty of room. Max keeps open house here.'

'I'd like to spend my last evening with my good-luck girl,' said Pete. 'Can you get the bike in the car or shall I follow on?'

'Cut out the "my girl",' said Anni, but they were all concentrating on the size of the little motorbike and whether it could be loaded aboard. It could, and was, although it reduced the seating space so that they had to cram in, and the jolting ride up the track to the villa was quite hilarious.

Climbing out at the journey's end, Anni smoothed down her skirt and ran her fingers through her hair and wished that Pete were somewhere else. Not only Pete; all of them. She wished she had been coming back alone, then she could go quietly into the house and look for Max and go to him, instead of being part of the crowd.

They weren't really that noisy, and there weren't that many of them, but they seemed to get between her and the man in the shadows of the big room while Henry was explaining that he had said it would be all right for Pete to stay overnight.

'Of course,' said Max. He looked at Pete, who said nothing, although his Adam's apple jerked in his throat as if he was trying to swallow.

'Pete's landed a super TV part,' said Jenny, 'and he came over to tell us about it before he leaves tomorrow.'

'He's got a captive audience here,' said Max, and Pete protested.

'I wouldn't be boring you like that.'

'On the contrary,' said Max, 'I shall insist on hearing all about it.' He sounded affable and he was smiling, and Anni was sure that nobody else realised that Pete was scared of him.

Now Pete was backing away and she said, 'He turned up out of the blue in the bay just now, full of this part he's landed. He's tickled pink with himself, he says it's his big break.'

Pete seemed to be fairly gibbering with excitement, and Max said drily, 'He's certainly giving a high-powered performance.'

'He is hamming it rather,' Anni had to admit, and she wished they were alone so that she could ask, 'Did you miss me today?'

Pete went on with his performance all evening, putting on the charm all round. At the dinner table he talked about the play. Not that he knew much about it yet, just that he had a starring role. Half the time when Max asked questions Pete's voice would trail off into a dry cough. He was not comfortable eye to eye with Max, and Anni wondered why he had wanted to spend another night under this roof when the master of the house could start him shaking by just looking at him.

She hoped he was not here because of her, that nonsense about a last evening with 'my good-luck girl', and she kept as aloof as she could without being too brusque. But when they decided to call it a day and trooped off to their rooms she found herself climbing the stairs with him.

With the others too. All except Max—he was locking up or something, still downstairs anyway. But on the gallery Pete's hand held her back as he looked down at Max and muttered, 'Does he wander round the house all night?'

'I don't know,' said Anni, 'but you'd better not,' and Pete grinned so that she added tartly, 'It isn't funny.'

He sobered quickly, the grinning face becoming anxious. 'You're right,' he said, 'it isn't.' He had seemed nervous and hyped up to her all evening, but now his confidence had completely deserted him and the star-to-be looked burned out. Was he scared that the play was going to flop and he was going to muff his chance?

'What's the matter?' she asked gently and he grinned again, fainter this time.

'Not a thing. You've got to grab your chances when they come, haven't you?'

'Sure you have,' she said. 'You do that,' and he kissed her hand with a flourish. 'See you in the morning,' she said as she got her hand back.

She watched him walk away and from down below Max called up, 'I suppose he could be Romeo but you don't strike me as Juliet.'

She put her hands on the balcony and struck a yearning attitude. Then she laughed. 'I don't strike me as Juliet either. By the way——' he was alone and the chance was too good to miss '—I got something for you today. Shall I fetch it?'

'Of course,' he said, and she hurried to her room and collected the little dish, wrapped in its gift paper.

'There's a message,' she said. 'See if you can crack the code.'

He could hardly miss the red rose and he said, 'Another rose?'

'You've got it. One from me because I've changed my mind, you can share my desert island.'

He said, 'We'll find one,' and that was when Abidin came up to Max talking Turkish that Anni couldn't follow. She stood around for a minute or two and then she murmured goodnight and Max said, 'Goodnight and thank you.'

'You're welcome. It's a date.'

On the gallery she looked down. The two men were still talking and, although from the tone of it they weren't discussing anything very important, Abidin had effectively ended her tête-a-tête with Max. A little longer and she might have found the courage to say, 'You can share my room tonight,' or Max might have said something else.

Now it would have to wait, although the very next chance she got she was going to get the message across.

* * *

Anni woke early. She had had no trouble from
Pete. Nobody had knocked at her door in the
night and she hadn't really thought that Max
might come. There were hours to go before breakfast but she was wide awake, and when she flung
her window open the air was clean and delicious.

She dressed and came out of the house. No one
was about yet, not even the staff, and she went
softly, disturbing nothing, into the gardens.

She had some idea that she might find Max here
or that he might see her from a window, and she
walked around the villa and back to the magnolia
tree and the gate in the wall that led on to the
mountainside. No one was following her and that
was a pity, but it was still a lovely morning and
she walked the way they had climbed, remembering where they had stood looking down on the
amphitheatre.

It was too early for tourists down there, too
early for anyone. She concentrated on recalling
the shape of rocks and trees and the changing
vista, and slowly she made her way up to the
slope that led to the little edge of the cave.

She was as delighted with herself as if she had
found a diamond mine. She pushed aside the
overhanging creepers and called 'Hello' and
listened. If there were echoes they were too faint
to reach her, but as soon as she stepped inside she
could hear the spring bubbling and by now she
needed the cool water.

She hadn't set off to come here. But when she
started walking it had become a game, following
the clues, and as she got nearer excitement had

quickened in her so that at the end she had been smiling when she called 'Hello'.

And got no answer, not even an echo, because the cave was empty and Max was not waiting for her.

'Sometimes I sleep up here,' he had said, and that had been at the back of her mind for a while so that she had almost expected to find him here. She knew that the odds were against it, but the let-down was like a cold wind blowing and she thought, I must stop looking for him all the time.

Because it was going to end. She couldn't stay here forever and Max would go away and what would it be like when she got back home if she couldn't enter a room or walk down a road without thinking, Maybe he's near? Because he would not be, not once in a thousand times. It was like reading that old saying that Victorians used to carve on their sundials—It is later than you think—and she had the sensation of time running out. As though suddenly every minute mattered desperately and she should not be standing here, alone in the cave.

She had to get back to the villa. There they would be well into breakfast and, unless she had been left to sleep in, wondering where she was. Nobody would worry about an hour or so, they'd presume she was taking a walk, but an uncontrollable feeling of urgency had her slipping and sliding and made it hard to go down safely and steadily.

When she reached the gate in the wall she raced

across the garden into the house and hurried
through the salon to the terrace.

In here everyone seemed to be standing around
but Max. The breakfast buffet was laid but no one
held plates, only coffee-cups, and no one spoke
until Jenny asked in a high, shrill voice, 'Where
have you been?'

'Walking, up the mountain.'

'We thought you'd gone with Pete.'

'Gone where? Has Pete gone?' Something terrible had happened. 'He left early.'

Her voice faltered and Henry said harshly, 'Early
but not empty-handed. He took a file with him.'

'What?' She had no idea what they were talking
about.

'From Max's study.'

'The book?'

'No.'

'Then *what*?' Nobody answered and there was a
small explosion in her brain. 'Not the Helen
papers?' She looked at their faces and they all
looked the same. 'But how could he know about
them?'

'Somebody must have told him,' somebody
said.

They meant her and she gasped wildly, 'Not
me. I didn't.'

'He turns up here the day after Max tells you
about the jewels of Helen and leaves with the
papers,' said Henry, dogged as a detective totting
up evidence. 'That's got to be more than coinci-
dence. You've got to be the one who told him.'

'No. Where's Max?' He would believe her. He knew her so much better than they did.

'He's gone after you,' said Jimmy, and he put his coffee-cup down and stood back as if she had become a laboratory specimen. 'You're a strange girl, aren't you? That business about Max smuggling out the finds that could have landed him in real trouble, how deliberate was that?'

'You know I didn't mean——'

'Ah, but we don't know,' said Henry. 'We don't know much about you at all except that you seemed to have it in for Max from the start. It was almost as if you had a grudge against him.'

She couldn't deny it and she said miserably, 'I did, for a long time, but that was before I knew him. I haven't any more. Everything's changed.'

'What sort of grudge? What's Max ever done to you?'

'Nothing. Not really. It was stupid.' She was talking to Jimmy. 'But you remember that accident when my brother was killed?' Of course he remembered, something like that would stay in your mind forever. 'Well, Roger saved your lives, didn't he? He shouted a warning and the rest of you got away, and I know now that it was crazy but I always felt that Max shouldn't have lived when Roger died. I don't know why it was Max I resented and nobody else, except that he was always so successful and I kept hearing about him and I kept thinking that Roger was just as clever. Roger could have been just as famous if he hadn't hesitated for that split second to warn the others.'

There was absolute silence and Jimmy then asked, very quietly, 'Who told you that?'

'Max told us.'

'Then Max lied. He was the one who shouted the warning. Roger freaked, he didn't move and nobody could have saved him, but it was Max who saw it coming and it was thanks to him that the rest of us got away.'

A lie to comfort a heartbroken man. 'My father thought he was a hero,' Anni whispered.

'Well, he wasn't,' Jimmy said savagely. 'Rog was a nice enough guy, but he was no hero and he was no genius either. He'd never have measured up to Max if he'd lived to be a hundred.'

Seeing Anni's stricken face, Jenny tugged at her husband's arm. 'Honey,' she pleaded, but for once Jimmy took no notice of her. He was too angry to stop; his voice shook with rage.

'So if this is some sort of private vendetta you've been operating here, Anni or Annabel or whatever your name is, you'd better tell lover-boy to get those papers back because you are playing way out of your league.'

'I can't tell him anything,' Anni wailed. 'I don't know where he is.'

'Is that a fact?' Jimmy looked as if he was about to shake information out of her when Henry stepped between them.

'Leave her till Max gets back.' Henry seemed to have taken over for the moment. 'We'd better go down to the launch as usual, we don't want to make too much of this yet. Suppose Philippe and

I go down and you two stay here.' He gave Anni a scathing sidewards glance. 'Keep her here.'

Anni said, 'I'm going nowhere.

'Too true you are not,' muttered Jimmy. 'Except back to your room.'

Someone followed her upstairs, and as she closed the door Jimmy opened it, took out the key and locked it from outside. Instinctively she rattled the knob but she knew that nobody was listening and she would probably have locked herself in anyway. Until Max got back she had nothing to say, and when he did come she could only say, 'Trust me.'

He hadn't trusted her. When the loss of the file had been discovered, and Pete had gone and she had gone, Max had accepted that she was in cahoots with Pete. Which meant that this week had counted for nothing. She had been so sure that she had a friend for life in him. She had longed for a lover but she had thought she had a friend, and a friend would surely have given her the benefit of the doubt.

Although that was not reckoning on the kind of life he led, among the cruelty and the treachery and the madness of the world. Nothing would surprise him—he was a cynical man who faced the facts, and the facts were against her. She had brought Pete here and she couldn't prove she had told him nothing.

She wondered what Pete would do with the papers and knew there were plenty of options. It would be a scoop any newspaper would pay handsomely for. Archaeologists would go spare and museums would vie for possession. Collectors with limitless funds would be bidding. And most horrific of all, even broken up, the gold melted down, the gems torn from their settings, the jewels of Helen could still make a man rich for life.

If she could get her hands on Pete she would half kill him, and why this when his big break had just turned up? Only it hadn't, had it? Not in acting. Somehow he'd heard about the file and he'd used the story of a TV part as an excuse for coming back for another night in the villa.

Now they were blaming her because she didn't know a two-timing snake when she saw one. Neither had they, but Pete was supposed to be her lover, and she was the one he had been embracing on the quayside and hand-kissing on the gallery. What did Max think Pete had been whispering in her ear up there? 'Tonight's the night, chicken, you play dumb and I'll meet up with you later.'

Then she had run downstairs with the rose dish and if Abidin hadn't appeared she might have spent the night with Max, and from the cynical way Max's mind worked he might have thought she was setting up an alibi for herself.

She wondered if he could have caught up with Pete and knew that it wouldn't happen yet. Pete would be gone like greased lightning as soon as he got his hands on that file, and he had had hours to keep going.

She could imagine him wheeling his bike down the mountainside until he was far enough away to

risk the sound of the engine, all the time looking
back for lights to go on in the villa and the chase
to start. He must have been terrified. Courage was
not his thing. No wonder he'd been nervous all
evening, knowing what he had planned.

She hoped he was counting the cost now if he
got clean away. He was greedy and money was
the prize, but, as Jimmy said, he was out of his
league robbing Max Torba, who would catch up
with him in the end. Although in the meantime
Pete could have blown the work of years and
ended a dream for Max. And for Anni. For Anni
the dream was over.

For now she was a prisoner. The door was
locked and the window was high and she would
have to be desperate to leap for the giant climbing
honeysuckle. If she did get down without breaking her neck the man working in the gardens
below might have orders to stop her. And where
did she think she could go?

More than anywhere else in the world, she
thought, I would like to hide in the cave, to make
a lair of it, to get away from everybody because
whatever I do goes wrong, and if I could find a
bolt-hole I would never come out again.

When the key turned in the lock she jumped
up. She had been sitting by the window for a long
time. The door opened and Jenny said, 'Come on,
he's back.'

'How did he get on? Did he catch up with—
Pete?'

She wanted to spit when she said Pete's name
but Jenny said, 'I don't know. The car's just drawn

up,' and went ahead quickly, avoiding talk, avoiding Anni.

They came down the stairs as Max came into the house. Jimmy had gone out to meet him and Jenny had fetched Anni. Max looked across at her as she stood near the bottom of the stairs.

He was grim as a hanging judge. Dark and powerful and cruel, and he thought she was as guilty as hell. 'Why?' he said.

Jimmy said derisively, 'You're not going to believe this, but this is Mafia stuff. A blood feud. This girl has a vendetta going against you. She thinks you caused her brother's death.'

Max's head jerked towards Jimmy. *'What?'*

'Seems you told his old man that Rog shouted the warning and little sister decided he died saving you. She wasn't too bothered about the rest of us, but she felt you had no right to the good life. So anything she could do to bring you down was fair game.'

It sounded insane and it had been crazy and Max said, 'What with one thing and another you are a very mixed up lady.'

She wanted to say, 'I was until I met you. I'm wiser now. I'm not much happier because you are letting me down with every word you say, but I'm not crazy any more.' She said, 'Would I have told you that and would I be here if I'd known what Pete was up to?'

'I don't know,' said Max. 'But if you felt that badly about me you could be enjoying this.'

'I could. I wonder why I'm not. Whether you

believe me or not I didn't know he was going to steal the papers and I didn't tell him about them.'

But suddenly she remembered, after the *jandarma* had gone through the house, telling Pete, 'He must have something that's pretty hot because he was saying nobody's getting hold of his papers.' She bit her lip and Max asked silkily, 'Something slip your mind?'

'I said you were working on something that was hush-hush, I did say that. But I said nothing about your search for the jewels of Helen. I hadn't seen him again till he turned up down in the bay, so how could I tell him?'

'There was time,' Jenny chipped in. 'By the way, did you phone your office yesterday?'

'What?' She had forgotten that excuse. 'No.'

'You didn't meet Pete and make any plans? You just went shopping? I don't remember any packages. What did you buy?'

'A dish.'

'Not much to show for a day round the markets,' said Jenny, who thought she had spent the day with Pete and had seen his arms around her when the dinghy came in.

Max had walked to the bottom of the stairs where he could look into Anni's eyes as she stood two steps up, clutching the handrail so that her knuckles whitened. 'He knew how you felt about me?' he asked.

'Yes.' She could feel the colour burning her cheeks. Pete knew. Not that she hated Max, but that she was falling for him, and much good that had done her.

'Do you think he did this to please you?'

'No.' If she had agreed to join Pete he might have tried to draw her into it, but this was for number one, Pete Hartley, small-time actor.

Max's voice was quiet. She knew he was looking into her face still, although she looked away, and he said, 'We can forget about the TV offer, that would be so much eyewash, but who is his agent?'

'I don't think he ever told me.'

'And you such very good friends?' That was said with heavy sarcasm. 'Who else are his friends?' She shook her head. 'His home address?' She kept shaking her head. 'I've been in touch with the Connollys. They put him ashore in Rhodes. Who did he know there?'

'I don't *know*.'

'Where was he staying in Idessa?'

He was renting a small apartment but she had never been back to it and she said raggedly, 'I don't know that either. And we're not old friends. I know I said we were but he picked me up that first evening, before I came here. He said he thought we'd met, and it was a corny line but I suppose we might have done somewhere and I'd forgotten. As far as I was concerned we were meeting for the first time.'

'Now that's going to be hard to argue with,' said Max, almost as if he were paying her a compliment. 'Total loss of memory. You know nothing about anything.'

She looked at him with mute appeal but she knew he was out to break her, and he said, 'But you've got to admit it's too handy to be true.'

He put an arm around her shoulders in a mockery of a protective gesture, yanking her fingers from the banisters, forcing her to go with him up the staircase. 'So let's call you a hostile witness,' he said, 'and see if a little shock treatment might cure your amnesia.'

CHAPTER SEVEN

'AND what got you up so early this morning?'
Max could have been asking Anni that as a cheerful enquiry, if his hand had not been like an iron
band gripping her arm and he had not been almost
dragging her upstairs.

'I woke, and it seemed a lovely morning and I
went for a walk.'

'Didn't sleep too well?' If she had had the least
idea what Pete was up to she would never have
closed her eyes. That was what he was suggesting,
although if she had had any inkling at all she
would have stopped Pete somehow. As it was she
had slept soundly until her brief nightmare, and
she wondered if she had been dreaming of Troy
burning while Pete was sneaking off with the
Helen papers.

She parted her lips to say, 'I dreamt——' but
Max's grim profile silenced her. This was no time
to start babbling about dreams, nor did she ask
'Where are we going?' as he marched her along
the corridor.

Up here were his study, and her bedroom
where he might be about to search her luggage for
clues. There was nothing to find, of course. She
hadn't even kept up her diary recently, and what
she had written had been only a journalist's
notebook.

136

She didn't think he was likely to get rough, although this was no gentle grip, and she said, 'I'm coming, aren't I? You can let go.' When he released her she rubbed her arm and muttered, 'You don't know your own strength.'

'Oh, yes, I do,' he said, 'and you would do well to remember it.'

He took her to the study. The door was slightly ajar and she asked, 'Don't you lock it?'

'I didn't think I needed to. I didn't realise I had a thief in my house.'

He meant her as well as Pete, and again colour she couldn't control flamed in her face, although it might be making her look guilty.

An open drawer in the desk by the window must have been where the papers had been filed, and she was sure that Pete had talked around, quoting her about the secrecy of something Max Torba was working on here. And somebody, a rival, an enemy, had said, 'Go get 'em.'

Until he was away with the papers he might not even have realised what he had got. She asked, 'What was in the file?'

'Addresses. Data.'

'Enough for someone to get ahead?'

'More neck and neck, but I'd prefer to stop him before then. I've reached the stage where I don't want fools rushing in.'

She clenched her stomach muscles, holding down hysterical laughter at the thought of Pete finding himself neck and neck with Max, although heaven knew she had nothing to laugh at.

Last time she had been in here during the

jandarma business Max's sense of humour had let her off the hook, but not for a second time. After hearing what Jimmy had to tell him he had decided she had been playing a hostile role all along, and now he was treating her as an enemy.

'Sit down,' he said, 'this could be a long session,' and his voice could not have been colder.

When she tried to explain, 'I did resent you after the accident but——' he cut her off with a gesture, but she felt as if he had clamped a hand across her mouth.

'Your opinion of me couldn't interest me less,' he said. 'You can blame me for World War Two for all I care. All I want from you is where that moron took my papers.'

'I don't *know*.'

He went on as if she had not spoken. 'He may have headed back to Rhodes. I've put it around there that I'm interested in him because he left my house with some of my property. I went to the restaurant where you introduced him to us. If I remember——' of course he remembered '—you told me you were travelling together.'

'We weren't.'

'Then why did you say you were?'

'Because you were warning me off the men.' She shrugged helplessly. 'I was mad at you. And it was something to say. But I had only met him the night before.'

'And he spend that night with you?'

'We were not lovers. We weren't even very good friends.'

Max's expression was weary with disbelief and

she said passionately, 'You don't believe me? Well, here's something else you are not going to credit. Pete was not my lover and I have never had a lover.'

When he drawled, 'And how do you propose to prove that?' she nearly said, 'Try me,' she was so desperate to stop this inquisition.

Saying that would have been real madness. He didn't want her and she was realising now that loving him could have finished her. Between them, her father and Robert had destroyed her pride so hurtfully that all the glamour and success she had achieved over the years had not brought enough confidence to let her give herself freely to any man since.

Until such a little time ago. Last night, this morning, she would have gone willingly to Max, but he had no real tenderness in him. This man who was smiling his tiger's smile and whose eyes were dark as the pit as he said, 'You're telling me you're a virgin?'

'Yes.'

'So am I.'

'What?'

'Do I look like a virgin?'

He looked what he surely was, a man of the world and many affairs, and she said bitterly, 'You look as if you've seen it all and done it all.'

'Not quite all,' he said, 'but nearly. But neither do you, my dear, look like a virgin.'

Even now she could start laughing hysterically. She said, 'And if I had to prove it I probably couldn't. What with riding and swimming and

generally hurtling around I've been pretty ener-
getic in every other respect.'

'That I can vouch for,' he said. 'But I don't
believe that a woman with your face and body
and your highly accomplished line in seduction
has reached twenty-six always saying no.'

Somehow she had always managed to distance
herself in time and she said, wryly, 'I'm frigid, I
guess. It must put them off when they get too
close.'

It was going to be true again, the ice was back
in her heart, and he said, 'You've been lucky.
Meeting men who take your word that the goods
that are displayed so temptingly are not on offer.'

'Haven't I just?'

'Pete Hartley did?'

'Yes.'

'Even after he came to your room that night?'

He had seen Pete go into her room, not leave,
and she said, 'I told you what happened then.'

She had told him so much the morning after,
and she had thought that after the week that
followed he would have trusted her, but she had
been wrong. An eyebrow rose in scepticism as he
drawled, 'No encouragement at all, and he's still
infatuated.'

'Is he?'

'But he is a very stupid man.'

'Thanks a lot.' Pete was not all that stupid. He
was quite cunning in a foxy way.

'He said nothing about his plans?' Max
persisted.

She shrilled back on a rising note, 'No, no, *no*!'

'All the same he might think they'd impress you. He might contact you.' Not by phone, there wasn't a phone. 'He might even risk coming back for you,' and her exasperation exploded.

'Of *course* he won't. He might fancy me, but it's nothing to the way he feels about you. You scare him witless. He thinks you could be a killer.'

'He could be right,' said Max, 'but I take your point. I can't see him strolling back here. So it looks as if I'll have to go after him.'

He leaned forward in his chair and it was as though his hands cupped her head so that she could not turn aside. When she found her voice this time it was flat and lifeless. 'I didn't tell him what the papers were. If it wasn't just a lucky dip someone else must have put him up to it. You've got enemies, haven't you?'

'More than I can count,' he said wryly, and today he had added her to the list and she wished she could hate him again. This would be easier then, but all she felt now was hopeless and helpless as though her life force were draining away.

'You insist that you met him for the first time after you arrived here,' he said, 'but you spent time together afterwards. What did he talk about?'

'Half the time I wasn't listening. He's the kind you don't listen to much.'

'Let's have the half when you were listening. Start when you say he picked you up.'

'Must I?'

He spoke deliberately and slowly, an acid edge to every word. 'If there was any other way I would not be sitting here with you. On all the evidence you are a liar but at the moment you're my only link with my light-fingered laddo and him I want.'

He seemd to be shouting at her although his voice had dropped lower. 'And if you don't start talking I swear I will get a truth drug into you.'

She shrank back. 'Don't touch me.'

'There's nothing I feel less inclined to do, except waste more time. So, where do you say you met him?'

'When I arrived in Idessa I booked into a little hotel, overlooking the harbour.'

'Name?'

She tried to remember, 'Something like Portan, Kortan, I'm not sure. I was sitting outside and Pete came up.'

Behind closed eyelids she could see it all again, how she had looked towards this way at the darker sky over Nidus thinking of Max Torba, telling herself that she hoped he would not be around when she came searching for the city under the sea. Yet next morning she had climbed up to the villa as if it was the man who brought her here.

She repeated Pete's words. 'He said, "Haven't we met before?" and it could have happened.'

'What did he tell you about himself?'

The TV ads, the shows. Pete had not been covering his tracks then so that was probably true, although she would no longer have accepted Pete Hartley's word on anything.

'This apartment of his.'

'I told you, I never went there.'

'Why not?'

'Because I didn't want to start an affair and that was obviously what was on his mind.'

'You'd know, of course,' said Max. 'But that was as far as your sixth sense went—you didn't suspect he was a con-man?'

'No, I didn't, and how do you want me to tell this? As it happened, or shall I just sit here while you fire questions at me?'

'Carry on,' he said.

'Well, next day he was where you met him, but I think he'd seen me with Jenny before and followed us. I was almost sure I saw him once or twice, that's why I think he turned up.'

'And the following morning he came out to the launch, where you told him and the *jandarma* that I was skimming off the finds. What did he tell you?'

'Nothing that I remember, about himself.'

'You went to him next morning while the police were questioning me?'

'I caught the bus and he was sitting at the table. I didn't really go to meet him.'

'And?'

'Nothing really. We went sightseeing.'

She didn't want to live it again, but he took her through day after day for any scrap of information she could dredge up about Pete Hartley.

There wasn't much. The clearer the memory of her time with Pete, the more vividly she recalled how Max had been on her mind even then. But she recounted everything else she could remember, even to how broke Pete was so that she was constantly paying out. She sounded gullible, a soft touch, and she said, 'I didn't mind. It was like having a girlfriend who was short of cash.'

'Hardly,' said Max drily. 'Whatever he was he was not in drag.'

'Oh, you know what I mean.'

He sighed. 'It would take a trained psychiatrist to know what you mean,' and that was not fair. She was doing her best to help him get back his wretched papers.

'Then you'd better get me a shrink,' she said wildly, 'and maybe I should be analysed because I don't know why I didn't listen to what he was telling me. You think I'm lying but I have got a genuine memory block, and if you've got any truth serum that you're set on trying I'll take it in a double vodka.'

After he'd listened to that outburst his voice and his face were expressionless. 'Do you want to remember or are you holding back?'

'Of course I want to remember.' She wanted Pete Hartley found so that she could get away from Max Torba.

'Will you let me hypnotise you?' he said, and something very cold ran the full length of her spine.

She licked lips that were suddenly dry and croaked, 'Could you do that?'

'If you go along with it. Without drugs it's almost impossible to hypnotise anyone against their will, but if you don't fight me we might get something out of your subconscious.'

She knew what was in her subconscious. Pete

had said things she had only half heard and of
which she had no recall, but she had been dreaming of Max loving her for the last few days at least.
If he got into her mind, regressing her so that she
was back before all this had happened, he would
learn how she had hungered for him. Although it
was only in dreams, it would be stripping herself
naked again for a man who had a heart of stone,
and she said stonily, 'I don't like the idea.'

'No?' He knew she was hiding something, and
she wondered if it would be possible to censor
what came back to her when she was being told it
was all coming back.

She said, 'I wouldn't make a good what-do-you-
call-it.'

'Do you know that?' She should have said that
it had been tried and it made her ill or something.
But she shook her head and he went on, 'Nine
out of ten can by hypnotised, and, the more
intelligent you are, the better subject you'd be.
Most folk can be hypnotists up to a point with a
little practice. There's no black magic in it.'

He was taking the mystique out of it because he
wanted her to relax and co-operate, but she said
stubbornly, 'It wouldn't work.'

'Shall we try a test?'

She said, 'No,' as he got up and came towards
her where she pressed her back against the back
of the chair, stiff and resistant.

'What are you afraid of?' he asked.

'I've never been hypnotised before. I don't like
the thought of losing control.'

'No one will be controlling you. You'll just

remember what you might have forgotten.' She chewed on her lower lip, and he said, 'I shouldn't think you need reassuring that I'm not likely to be taking any physical advantage of you.' That certainly hadn't crossed her mind. She was not that conceited or that stupid.

'What sort of test?' she said.

'Clasp your fingers together.' She joined her hands, fingers locking. 'As I count ten,' he told her, 'your grip will tighten. At each count your fingers will become more tightly clenched.'

He counted slowly, one. . .two. . .three. . . with seconds between each, and she looked down at her clasped hands lying in her lap, and the muscles and nerves were tensing and tightening until her nails dug deep into the back of her hands.

When he said, 'Ten,' they were clamped so rigidly there was hardly any sensation in them. 'Your hands are locked,' he told her. 'You can't open them no matter how hard you try. Try to move your fingers.'

She couldn't. They wouldn't even twitch. He could have stuck pins in her and she probably wouldn't have felt it. She stared down at them horrified and he said, 'I shall count to ten again and as I do your grip will loosen. Slowly your hands will relax.'

Again her fingers obeyed his voice, and when he said ten they fell apart. 'Good,' he said. 'You'd make a first-class subject.'

She had been hoping to show that she would be a rotten subject, but she had been given no choice, and if it was true that you couldn't be hypnotised against your will it had to mean that she had no defences. That she couldn't fight him. If he said, 'Your eyelids are heavy, you are very tired, and you are sinking down into sleep, going back. . .' the next thing she knew she would be lying on a sundrenched beach, with Pete still no more than a droning voice, pretending that Max was with her, calling for Max.

'No, thank you,' she said. 'If you can do that to my hands, what would you do to my head?'

'This isn't mental rape.'

'So you say.'

She shied away as if his touch could scald her, and he said, 'All right, it obviously isn't going to work.'

'It scares me. Maybe there is more I could remember and if I go away something might come to me. I'll make notes, shall I?'

'Why not?'

'I do want to help.'

'I don't doubt it,' he said. 'The question is whom?' He thought it was Pete she was helping, and, although she walked steadily out of the room and down the corridor, as soon as she closed her bedroom door she got the shakes again. She sat on the edge of the bed for a few minutes before her agitation subsided, but she still felt as if she had fallen out of a spin-drier.

Max didn't think that her 'help' was going to be much use, although she must have given him some information about Pete. He had his sources, he would track Pete down, but by then Pete could

have struck a deal and the file could have changed
hands, and she should not be sitting here, trying
to remember what she had never heard. She
should be looking for somebody who knew Pete.

She had said she didn't know any of his friends,
and nor did she, but there were folk he had
exchanged greetings with while he was with her.
She hadn't met them, it had just been a 'Hi', as
Pete had kept her to himself, but when he was
not with her he wouldn't be mooning around on
his own. He was a charmer and a sponger; he
would be where the money was being spent.

It was much easier to think clearly when she
was away from Max. He was a professional, but
he thought she was a liar and a cheat. He devastated her at every turn, reducing her to emotional
rubble.

Now she was away from him she could begin to
think calmly about what had happened while she
was with Pete. For instance, in Idessa when they
sat outside Kortan's. Pete drinking *raki*, she with
fruit juice telling him about the police raiding the
villa. Now she remembered how, as they got up
to leave, two men at another table had nodded
and smiled as if they knew him. If she saw those
men again she might recognise them.

She was wishing that she had been less stand-
offish because then Pete might have confided in
her, or tried to get in touch with her later. He
could have left the country by now, but if he was
still around, and she was seen to be alone, perhaps there was the faintest chance he might turn
up again.

If she went back to Idessa she might learn something. Anything was worth trying. She picked up her handbag and was passing the open door of the study, rummaging in her bag for a tissue, when Max walked out full pelt into her.

It could have been chance or he might have seen her and moved like lightning, but there was a small collision with the contents of her handbag spilling at her feet. She thought he was helping her as she gathered lipstick, mirror, comb, purse, but then she saw that he had only picked up her little travelling address book and her passport.

Still on her knees, she stared up speechless as he flicked over the pages of the small book. 'No Hartley,' he said.

She was furious enough to snap, 'I've got a much bigger book at home with a lot more names in.'

'Of course you have,' he said.

'May I have it back?' He finished going through it while she seethed silently. When he handed it over she dropped it into her bag and held out her hand again, but he slipped her passport into his pocket and she demanded incredulously, 'Am I under house arrest?'

'Put it this way,' he said, 'I have a gut feeling you're not telling me all you know and I don't intend parting company with you until you do.'

'You have no right——' Somehow she stopped herself raging on. 'But of course you know that, only it's Torba's law for now, isn't it?'

She had been going downstairs, to try to discuss her idea with one of the others, but she was damned if she would lift a finger to help after this. She was not on Pete's side, he was a miserable little sneak-thief, but she was not on Max Torba's side either. To hell with both of them.

Anger was warming her up again. The threat of the third degree going on and on and the indignity of having her passport pocketed so coolly made her say furiously, 'You can't keep me here; if I want to go I go.'

He was actually laughing at her, and she went to grab or hit—to get her passport back or stop him laughing—and he caught her raised arm by the wrist. 'I hit back,' he warned her.

'I bet you do, but do you ever pick on anyone your own size, or can't you find anyone?'

'You measure up pretty well,' he said, which was ridiculous when she was being lifted almost off her feet.

'If I don't get my passport I shall raise an almighty stink.'

'Who'll hear you?'

She lurched as he loosed her, then she leaned against the wall and glowered at his broad back as he walked away down the corridor.

The little book contained the names of folk she usually sent cards to on holiday. But this holiday she had written to nobody. No one would be certain where she was, and that was her own fault for forgetting them because they were the best friends she had. Not a lover among them, but she could have done with any one of them here now.

She went out into the garden well away from the house. Nobody spoke to her out here, but she

felt as if she was still under supervision. The man
who was tending the flower-beds could have been
engrossed in his work, but she was sure he would
have intercepted her if she had headed for the
gates. Just inside the main entrance another man
leaned on a broom, or swept slowly, raising dust.
And she did see Abidin watching from a window.

It was not past Max to give orders that she was
confined to the villa, and if she tested her theory
by walking through the gates there could be an
unpleasant little scene. She had had enough
unpleasantness today so she stayed within the
high white walls, wandering around for a while,
then sitting on the low marble wall round the
fountain, trailing her fingers in the water, racked
with bitter regrets.

There was plenty to regret. She wished she had
never phoned Max Torba, never come here, never
heard of the jewels of Helen. She remembered the
fantasy they had played in the amphitheatre when
he had pretended to deck her in fabulous splen-
dour, and the only jewellery she was really wearing was a single earring.

She was still wearing it, and she yanked it out
of her earlobe and tossed it into the water. For a
moment she thought she had splashed her face
before she realised why her cheeks were wet.
Almost at once the sun dried her tears and,
whatever else happened to her, she must never
do that again.

So what was she to do? By the time the Range
Rover came back from the bay, and Henry and
Philippe went into the house, she had made her

plans, but she stayed outside until Jenny came
looking for her. 'Come and eat,' Jenny said, and
Anni followed her into the sumptuous little
dining-room.

As the others were seating themselves she
looked at Max. 'I'm sure you don't want to eat
with me and I'll stand less chance of choking if I
take a plate up to my room. Do you mind?'

'Try the soup,' he said. 'I don't want you
choking.'

'Not until you've brought on the thumbscrews?'
She scooped haphazardly from salad dishes and
turned on the way out to look at them all and say
witheringly, 'You've all got sky-high IQs so how
is it you are all so thick?'

It was maddening that they wouldn't understand how she might help if she had been treated
differently, because she was pretty sure that if she
could get into Idessa she could find somebody
who knew where Pete had been staying. She
could try to leave a message for him—'Would you
say Anni was here? Ask him to ring me.'—and
she would find a number that he could call.

But she wouldn't tell any of them, least of all
Max, who would frighten Pete so that he would
never stop running. If she made any sort of
contact she would decide then how to go from
there. The papers had been stolen, a criminal
offence for which she was partly responsible, and
she owed it to herself to do *something*.

Sitting under the honeysuckle tree under her
bedroom window, she had waited until, with any
luck at all, they were safely gathered in for the

evening, but it was still early enough for tourist traffic along the road to Idessa. And she had money, she would get herself into the little town.

'If I want to go I go,' she had told Max, and he had laughed and held her squirming and that had been an out-and-out challenge. She was hunting Pete Hartley, but the excitement would be in outwitting Max. Showing him that holding her passport did not mean holding her. Maybe in the morning she would wait for them down in the harbour. But wherever she faced Max Torba again she would be free of him and that would be a real triumph.

She locked her door, although she knew that nobody was likely to come looking for her before morning. Then she changed the white shirt she had been wearing for a shirt in moss-green, as she didn't want to be conspicuous on the mountain-side, and zipped money and the door key into her jeans pockets.

There were back stairs, but they led through the kitchens where she would be bound to meet someone. The gardens seemed deserted. She stood at the window until she was sure there was nobody about. Earlier she had looked up into the giant honeysuckle for a way down and tonight she was both desperate and determined. Now she leaned out of the window, reaching for one of the twisted boughs, gripping and swinging herself up, legs wrapping around. Keep-fit exercises paid off, she was agile and supple, and she came through the tangle of perfumed foliage dishev-elled but unscathed, landing lightly and staying down while she looked around.

Rows of windows overlooked here but no one seemed to be watching and she ran, keeping low and using all the cover there was. The main gates were open and she held her breath, running hell for leather through them out on to the track that led down to the road to Idessa.

It would have been easier staying on the track, but from the top windows of the villa her moving figure might still be spotted, and now she could identify in a warped fashion with Pete. He had been fleeing Max Torba's wrath and so was she. Although if she was caught it would only be her pride that would suffer. Pete would be worried about getting his good looks roughed up.

Come to that, if she caught up with Pete herself she would be tempted to hit him with something heavy, but it was no fun coming down a mountainside never daring to look back. She kept beside the track but not on it, although this ground was rougher, with fissures and tangled undergrowth, and she couldn't help thinking of snakes. More than once she stumbled and once she was almost brought to her knees.

There were houses and fields near the road, but up here was wilderness and it would not have taken much to convince her that she was being shadowed. There was no sound of following footsteps, no shadow fell across her path, but a feeling of pursuit was quickening her pace until she was gasping for breath and hurtling along. And again her foot turned, slithering between stones, and this time she went full length.

There was no pain, she hadn't twisted anything

that mattered. But she lay face down, eyes closed, with the bracken scratching her skin, because this was a warning that she had to go slowly. She could break a leg and lie there till morning.

'I presume you are just getting your breath back,' said Max, and that galvanised her so that she shot up and round.

He swore softly and she shrieked, 'Sorry I haven't broken my neck, was that what you were hoping for?'

'I'm cursing myself, not you,' he said wearily. 'Where are you meeting him?'

Her mind was spinning, but she knew now why she had been let loose. Max thought she was in touch with Pete and that she could lead him to his quarry and she went on shrieking, 'If you wanted me to make a break for it why did you take my passport? Or was that to fool me?'

'That was an impulse. I didn't want you leaving the country, but I didn't consider impounding your passport until it fell at my feet.'

Like you, his expression said, as he looked down at her where she was still slumped. She had been sure that the next time they met she would be the cool one, and she sat up straight, scowling at him. He had been trailing her from the start and she wondered how he would have followed her into Idessa and had no doubt that he would. He could have had a car waiting down in the bay. As she walked through the streets he would have been there, and she said tartly, 'Aren't you on the big side for shadowing? Wouldn't one of the others have merged in better?'

'I'm a great believer in doing my own dirty work.'

'Well, you've done for this job, haven't you?'

He came round and sat down beside her. 'Looks like it,' he said, and there was no point in running now. She would just have to sit here until she got her breath back. She should be furious that she had been set up and gone through all this for nothing. But he had gained nothing either, and he had blown his cover because he had thought she might have hurt herself.

'Anyway,' she said, 'I wasn't going to meet Pete. I was going to try to find him.'

'How?' he asked as if he was mildly curious, and she shrugged.

'Oh, ask about. I thought I might find somebody who knew something and I might get a message to him.'

'What message?' He sprawled, loose-limbed and relaxed, and she sat hunched, chin resting on her knees.

'I don't know,' she said irritably. 'I hadn't got that far.'

'You've changed your tune. Earlier you said there wasn't a hope in hell he'd contact you.'

'Not if you were around, I said. If I were on my own he might have done, but unless you let me try we won't be knowing will we?'

She had thrust her face nearer his, and when he reached across and touched her hair her defensiveness nearly went up in a puff of smoke. But this was no caress; he pulled out a sprig of spiky grass and she told herself that the shock had been alarm bells ringing. Physically he was stunningly attractive, but she had learned her lesson there.

She raked her fingers through her hair, although it couldn't matter less if she had acquired the odd blossom and briar, climbing through the honeysuckle and falling face down just now.

'Tomorrow perhaps,' he was saying. 'I can keep tabs on you by daylight, but you're a slippery lady. With or without a passport I might lose you come nightfall.'

It sounded as if he didn't trust her, but he was prepared to take a gamble, and she asked, 'So what now?'

'We wait for morning. Now, at the risk of repeating myself, come on, baby, time to go home.'

Remembering when he had said that before stabbed at her heart, dragging a rasping half-sob from her throat as she jumped up, and she went down again, lying through her teeth, 'My ankle!'

'Fantastic,' he said. 'You swarm down the side of the house like a monkey and then you nobble yourself on open ground.'

'That was because I heard you coming after me.'

'You did?' He sounded surprised, and she had heard nothing. It had all been in her imagination, unless there *were* vibes that would always tell her when he was near. And that was nonsense; she was having none of that.

'Why do you think I started running?' she said.

She was holding her ankle, and when he stooped to lift her fingers her grip tightened instinctively. But she had to let him look and he said, 'It doesn't seem to be swollen.'

She would have been astonished if it had, but he pressed lightly around the ankle bone and she yelped, 'Ouch.'

'Can you walk?' She got to her feet with him supporting her, and then she put down her 'injured' foot and mimed agony, swaying back and grimacing.

'It's all right,' he said, 'I'll carry you.'

Having pretended her ankle had twisted, she had known she would have to limp a little, but now he was proposing giving her a lift up the mountainside she could have chortled with glee. He had let her make a fool of herself getting down here, and it would be rough justice if he made a fool of himself getting her back again.

There was quite a climb ahead of him. It would be interesting to see how far he got with her weight aboard, and nobody could prove that her ankle didn't hurt. Even if it didn't swell up she could have ricked a tiny tendon.

'Are you sure I'm not too heavy for you?' she enquired as he picked her up.

'I'm not sure about anything where you're concerned,' he said. 'But for the moment hang on and shut up.'

She had to clasp her hands around his neck so that she was looking straight into his face, and her lips trembled like a twinge of pain. In a way it was, and she turned her face away so that her cheek was pressed against his chest and she could hear his heartbeats.

They were steady enough, while her heart was throbbing a wild tattoo. This had not been a good idea but she couldn't change her mind yet about being able to walk.

He was getting into his stride, going steadily up the track at an even pace. She could feel the rippling muscles in the arms that held her, the long, strong legs climbing rhythmically and effortlessly, and she lay limply because she was trying not to react in any way. If she let sensation take over she would be the one who couldn't get her breath.

He was not breathless. He was breathing deeply and she moved with the rise and fall of his chest. She had to get her mind on to something else and she began reciting nursery rhymes in her head. Mary had a little lamb. Hickory dickory dock. Jack and Jill went up the hill—she nearly got the giggles over that one.

Then she ran through Portia's speech from the trial scene in the *Merchant of Venice*. She had seen that in Stratford last month, with a man with whom she had been getting on famously, only now she could hardly remember what he looked like.

A couple of Shakespeare's sonnets. A poem of Emily Brontë's. . . 'I cannot be more lonely, More drear I cannot be! My worn heart throbs so wildly 'Twill break for thee. . .'

That brought a lump to her throat. She thought those must be among the saddest words ever written and Emily must have been one of the loneliest of women.

Anni had always known what loneliness was, but never more bitterly than now, in the arms of a man who distrusted and despised her. She stiffened, tensing her shoulders and pulling back, and he stopped.

They were nearly there. He was as tough as he looked, he had almost got her up to the villa, and she said, 'I might manage from here.'

He set her down so that she was sitting and then he examined her ankle again, which was of course slim as ever although she gave a token intake of breath when he moved her foot.

He straightened up, taking her by both hands so that she stood too. 'We'll try a fireman's lift from here,' he said. He was not throwing her over his shoulder like a sack of potatoes, and she pretended to test her foot and grinned.

'I *can* manage.' She met his glare wide-eyed. 'I heal quickly.'

'You need to,' he said grimly, and he was fooled no longer. He knew she had made the climb back as hard as she could for him, and she gave up the charade, stepping out.

They finished the climb in silence, then in through the gates and into the house where everybody seemed to be in the salon. When Max said, 'Everything's in hand,' his expression was not encouraging and they asked no questions.

Now he had Anni by the arm and was marching her towards the staircase. She turned as she went and said cheerfully, 'You'll be surprised to hear he blew it, I heard him coming. Ah, well, better luck next time.' She looked at Max. 'Back to my room?'

'Next time you might not be so lucky with the honeysuckle,' he said. 'It's not exactly a climbing tree.'

'In that case would it be too much to ask for some supper? I didn't stop for dinner.'

'Neither did I.' They were at the top of the stairs and he called down from the gallery, speaking in Turkish, and Sezer hurried off in the direction of the kitchens.

'Are we having supper together?' asked Anni.

'We are.'

'Where?'

For answer he took her down the corridor, along another passage to a room she had never seen into before but which she knew was his bedroom. The bed dominated it, or seemed to at her first startled glance, and she said, 'If I'm not to be trusted alone, wouldn't it be easier to ask Jenny if she'll be gaoler for the night?'

He closed the door behind them. 'This is between you and me,' he said. 'Sleeping or waking tonight, I am not letting you out of my sight.'

CHAPTER EIGHT

'THAT could have its embarrassing moments,' said Anni.

'Not for me,' said Max. 'And I really can't believe that spending a night with a man will be a new experience for you.'

She was sorry now that she had admitted she was inexperienced. She would rather he thought she was unshockable, and she drawled, 'Depends what the man has in mind.'

He laughed then. 'All this man requires is your company, as you very well know. Not even conversation. Just the certainty that you will be here in the morning.'

'You wouldn't take my word for it?' He shook his head and she pulled a wry face, admitting, 'You could be right. It would be given under duress, and that sort of promise doesn't count. So, you're not letting me out of your sight, and so we come to the first very small embarrassment— where's the bathroom?'

He pointed to a door and she opened it and said, 'Of course, en suite, the master bedroom. May I shut the door?'

'Of course.'

'I've got to wash and I'd like to change and I shall need a toothbrush. Will you come with me to fetch them?'

Everything she needed was in her room and he said, 'I'll give you five minutes, I don't think you're likely to run just yet.'

She was beginning to feel that she would never run again, but she kept her voice light and amused. 'And I don't suppose you feel much like chasing me.'

'Not after carrying you back, no.'

She managed a grin as she sauntered out of his room, and was glad that she had put her key into her pocket instead of leaving it in the lock. She gathered up her toilet bag and a change of clothing, and was on her way back again before she wondered why she hadn't locked herself in her room.

He might have left her there, or again he might not, and she didn't want any more hassle. After she had showered and changed and eaten she should be able to cope, but for now she was shattered.

Max was a dark shape against the pale outline of a window and she didn't look towards him again. She went straight into the bathroom, past the huge bed. She could hardly have felt more exhausted if she had carried him up the mountain-side, and she stripped off her dust- and sweat-stained shirt and jeans and scrubbed herself under the shower, turning the dial to cold and waiting for the stinging water to refresh and revitalise her.

When she stepped out at least she was cleaner, but she still didn't feel over-bright. She had to stand on tiptoe to see her reflection in the bottom half of a shaving mirror, and she wished she hadn't bothered because she looked how she felt. She hadn't brought any make-up with her and until her hair dried it would hang limp and flat.

She left her shoes and came out barefoot—her feet were clean, her shoes were not and there were lights on now in the room. Someone must have brought up food because a small table was laid with two chairs drawn up.

Max sat there and Anni said, 'Cosy.'

When he looked at her it cleared her head more effectively than standing under the cold shower. There was nothing cosy about him or the situation, and now she was wishing that she had stayed in her own room. If she had barricaded herself in there wouldn't have been much he could do about that. Now she was locked in with him and she was going to need all her bravado to get her through the night.

She took her seat at the table and drank thirstily from her wine glass. Then she helped herself to food from the various dishes. He hadn't waited, he was eating, and she was hungry because all she had had today was two figs she had picked this afternoon. But now the food was in front of her the sight of it made her squeamish.

The buttered rice looked awfully rich, and she stabbed into a stuffed pepper and came up with a rubbery morsel. She got that down gulping the dregs of her wine and asked, 'What do you intend doing tomorrow?'

'Let's hear your plans.' He refilled her glass. 'What would you have done tonight, if you'd got away?'

He probably still thought she was off to meet Pete and she pointed out, 'I'd have come back tomorrow, wouldn't I? My passport's here, my luggage is here.'

'Just an overnight stay?'

'Yeah. Instead of which I've got an overnight stay with you.'

A glass and a half of wine on an empty stomach were perking her up. She put down her fork and held her glass in both hands, looking up at him over the rim. 'That will be something to tell your fans in my office. They'll be thrilled to hear about that. Max Torba and me, spending the night together.'

'You're sure you didn't hit your head when you fell?' he asked drily.

'Maybe I did.' She picked up her fork again and set about the rice because she had to be needing food. Between mouthfuls she told him, 'One thing I'd have done in Idessa was send a few cards home telling folk I was in your house, just in case you did intend chaining me up in the cellars.'

'Don't they know you're here?'

'No. I booked into a hotel, remember—I didn't intend staying here until you bullied me into it.'

'I didn't bully you.'

He sounded amused and she went on, 'Well, after I'd posted my cards I thought I would go back to where Pete picked me up, because there were a couple of men at one of the tables who seemed to know him.' Max nodded, registering that, and she was quiet for a moment, her luminous grey eyes narrowed and glinting and her jawline clean and hard. 'I want to find him,' she said softly.

After another brief silence Max said, 'I think you might. Or he might find you.'

'Come back for me, you mean?'

He said, 'Yes,' and she poured more wine for herself.

It was relaxing her so that she joked almost without thinking, 'Would you come back for me?' When he laughed she laughed too, it was that ridiculous. Then she said, suddenly solemn, 'But you're prepared to stake me out and wait in the shadows and see if the trap gets sprung. I don't like the sound of that.'

'Not fair play, you mean?' He was still laughing at her.

'Something like that.'

'Let's leave it for now.'

'Let's.' She sat back in her chair and waited, and then asked, 'So, what shall we talk about?'

'Anything you like.'

She thought. For something to say she came up with, 'Where did you learn to hypnotise?'

'I didn't. I was on an expedition in the Andes, there was a rock fall and one of the men got his leg shattered. I held his hand and told him it wasn't so bad, he was going to be fine, and he said the pain was going. As it happened he was fine, we got him down and the bones mended, and that was my introduction to the powers of suggestion.'

'Fascinating,' she breathed.

'Glad you think so. It all passes the time. Read any good books lately?'

'A few. And you?' More wine. 'Do you read Emily Brontë?'

'Not a lot.'

She rotated her glass very gently, the stem between her fingertips. 'Not a lot of fun, was it, life for the Brontë sisters?'

'Living in a churchyard can't have helped. No wonder Branwell took to the bottle.'

'What a good idea.' She raised her glass and toasted 'Branwell,' but it wasn't steadying her any more. The alcoholic kick had reached her brain in a rush and everything was beginning to blur. She looked at him as steadily as she could and said in a high voice, 'Well, I need something to get me through the night.'

Either he spoke very quietly or she was hearing woozily. 'You don't need to get stoned. I'm neither going to grill you nor assault you.'

'I know that, but you make me nervous.' Her teeth were starting to chatter now and she was jabbering. 'I don't want to sit here all night, twitching and talking rubbish. I'd rather sleep and see what tomorrow brings, and I can't sleep cold sober while you're watching me like a warder.'

He got up from the table, pushing back his chair. 'Take the bed and leave the bottle.'

'Thank you,' she said with exaggerated courtesy.

'It's that way.'

She knew where the bed was. She walked across with all the dignity she could muster and

lay down, turning her face away from the spinning room and the man who was sober as a judge.
She didn't care. She really did not care how
terrible she felt in the morning, so long as nobody
disturbed her until morning came.

But she woke before then. A lamp was burning
dimly on a table against a far wall, throwing the
room into shadows. She knew at once where she
was and that when she moved she could become
very fragile indeed. But she didn't have to move
her head, only her eyes to see that Max was lying
well away, taking up almost the full length of the
mattress.

'What are you doing in my bed?' she mumbled.

'It isn't your bed, Goldilocks, it's mine. Go to
sleep.'

That was easier said than done. Nausea was
churning in her stomach and a dull ache in her
head began pounding as her brain came painfully
back to life. What had started as a glass of wine to
keep up her courage had led to her making a
pathetic fool of herself. After this how was she
going to face the morning, let alone face Max?

He hadn't sounded as if he was sleeping, just
lying there resting and relaxed, and when morning came he would spring into action like a tiger
while she would hardly be fit to crawl. She almost
groaned aloud, but he would have heard that so
she lay still, suffering in silence, until she thought
she might just have the strength to drag herself
into the bathroom and search for aspirin or
something.

She had to get round the bed to reach the

bathroom door, and he saw her roll off the bed of course, feeling her way and going slowly to avoid any jolting. When she leaned against the wall and closed her eyes she knew he was watching her, and she said, 'I think I've got food poisoning.'

'Probably the mussels,' he said ironically. He got off his side of the bed and went into the bathroom and came back with a glass half full of a brackish-looking liquid. 'Drink this,' he ordered.

'What is it?'

'Just drink it.' It tasted foul. She gagged as she swallowed, so that emptying the glass seemed to take a long time, and then she was not sure she could keep it down. She swayed, hiccuping, a hand over her mouth.

'Do you use much of that?' she croaked.

'No, I keep it for friends. Now, come back to bed.'

'I'm not coming——' Her defiance was reflex, and ridiculous when she was almost dropping, and when he lifted her she flopped down and wriggled frantically over to 'her' side of the bed.

'What proof was it, that wine?' she asked, after a few minutes in which the nausea was subsiding, although her headache was still fierce.

'Average,' he said. 'You shipped a fair amount, but it shouldn't have knocked you out.'

'I hadn't eaten all day.'

'That wouldn't help.'

That poisonous-tasting concoction he'd brought her had helped, and he had helped her back into bed, and now he was lying not beside her but right over there and his voice was deep and quiet

and almost soothing. She might get to sleep again,
if only her head would stop throbbing.

Her face was against the cool bed covering so
that her voice was muffled. 'You know what you
did for the man with the broken leg? Well, how
are you with headaches? I'm sorry I lied about the
ankle, but I do have the most awful head.'

And then she was lying in the circle of his arms,
with his fingers lightly touching pressure-points
on her temples, between her brows. Gently,
gently, until the pain was ebbing away and drow-
siness was stealing over her. She sighed and
smiled as he stroked her hair, and then her eyes
closed and she slept, comforted, in Max Torba's
arms for all that was left of that night.

She woke when he said, 'Anni, wake up,' and the
room was full of light and he was bringing her
black coffee. 'How do you feel?' he asked as she
squirmed upright.

'Not too bad.' She grinned back, slightly shamefaced when he smiled, and took the coffee. 'Thank
you very much,' she said, thanking him for last
night's noxious brew as well as for cuddling her
to sleep. He had been kind and she was definitely
on his side again. Today she was going all out to
help get the papers back. She was hardly fighting
fit, but she was healthier than she expected to be,
and happier.

'Come down when you're ready,' he said.

'What time is it?'

'Just after nine.' He was shaved. The dark blue
shirt and the dark trousers were fresh clothing.

He must have been up and about while she had slumbered on, and he looked as if he had slept too—his eyes were clear and keen. Of course he would know she was secure enough while he had an arm around her, and she felt herself blushing scarlet and was glad when he went out of the room.

She was still well over on his side of the bed. The quilt was rumpled and pillows under it showed where heads had been—it was all pretty incredible. But reassuring. Today might not be so bad after all. She drank her coffee and used his bathroom, then went along to her own room to brush her hair and see what a little skilful make-up would do for a morning-after face.

She didn't hurry. He hadn't said hurry, and the slower she went, the stronger she felt, so that when she was fairly satisfied with her appearance she strode almost light-heartedly along the corridor.

The salon was empty as she came down the stairs, although she could hear voices through the open door of the city-room. She was walking towards them, passing the main door, when someone knocked on that hard enough to bring back memories of the *jandarma*.

While she stood, irresolute, Max came out of the city-room, Jenny and Philippe trailing behind him, and answered the door. Jenny squealed and ran, Philippe mouthed a Gallic oath, and Max said, 'Good morning, gentlemen.'

Anni froze as Pete and a man she didn't know

came into the house. Pete was rumpled, his carefully tended hair tousled, and his clothes looked
as if he had slept in them. He didn't meet Anni's
eyes. Or anyone's. He looked shifty as a cornered
rat, although not half as dangerous. Maybe a
cornered mouse.

The other man was not happy either. He was
short and stocky with thick coppery hair, blunt
features and tired eyes. There was a twisted grin
on his face as he faced Max. 'I'm Tom
McGonagall,' he said, as though he was apologising for it.

'I'm Max Torba. Is that my property?'

McGonagall was carrying a hefty envelope. He
handed it over and Max said, 'Thank you,' and
dropped it on a side table.

Philippe asked, 'You are checking?'

'Everything's here, or they wouldn't be,' replied
Max.

Everything about him was dangerous. Not just
his size and stance, but his voice and the sheer
power of his presence. As he looked at them the
other two men seemed to shrink.

And then Jenny was rushing back with Jimmy
and Henry who almost skidded to a halt, reaching
the others, staring at Pete. Henry roared, 'What
the blazes is going on?'

'The return of the loot.' Max indicated the
envelope, and, turning to Pete, he said quite
gently, 'Suppose you tell us what is going on?'

Pete gulped, his Adam's applie bobbing again,
and McGonagall said, 'I'll tell you. It's a barmy
business but there's no harm done, is there? Me,

I'm a freelance journalist, and I'm on holiday now—we've got a villa just outside Rhodes. I know Pete here,' he gave Pete a look that was far from friendly, although he went on, 'we've cracked a few bottles together in our time. And last week he was telling me you'd got papers here proving that the treasure from Troy wasn't broken up after the war. And I said they'd be worth a fortune and I'd give my eye-teeth to see the proof.' The glare he turned on Pete now was murderous. 'Next thing I know the stupid sod turns up with them.'

It seemed to be more than he could take; he shook his head like a punch-drunk boxer. 'Of all the crack-brained stunts to pull. I thought he was too streetwise for that. I took one look at them— that was all, not enough to tell me a thing except what they were. And I knew whose they were and I said, "Have Torba after me for the rest of my life? Not me, mate. He wouldn't need to put a hit-man on us, he's a hit-man himself."'

Anni had no doubt those had been his exact words and Max drawled, 'Kind of you to say so.' It was becoming ridiculous and she had to smile.

Pete suddenly found his voice and yelped, 'Stop grinning and tell him.'

He was looking at her, wide-eyed, and the smile was wiped off her face as she gasped, 'What?'

'Tell him that it was your idea. I did it for you.'

Max had suggested that, but stealing the papers had never been her idea. 'No,' she cried, and inside her skull her brain was whirling.

Pete sounded as if he had run a mile uphill,

panting for breath, gasping out, 'You came here gunning for him. You wanted to be in at the kill.' She had said something like that, a lifetime ago it seemed, but when he shouted, 'You told me to take the bloody papers!' that was never true and she yelled back.

'You are a liar.'

'I'm crazy about you.' He was crazy, all right, raving. 'You know I'd do anything for you. That's what this is all about.' He looked Max in the face for the first time and quickly back to Anni. He could meet her eyes without flinching, he was not frightened of her, and she was getting angrier at every word.

'If I'd got away with it you'd have been quick enough to cash in, wouldn't you? But I've been brought back so you'll have to settle for having had your fun for a day or two, laughing at him, laughing at me for being your push-over.'

He actually laughed, throwing back his head and pealing with theatrical mirth, and Anni hit him a stinging slap that shut him up. He clapped his hand to his cheek and she turned to Max, who said, 'I warned you, I hit back.'

'You can't believe him.'

His eyes were hooded and his voice was soft. 'Where's your proof that he's lying?' and she felt as if he had struck her.

She said brightly, 'Ah, there's the rub, and you've already told me you don't take my word. Still, I'm glad you've got them back, the joke was wearing a bit thin. Everybody happy now?' She smiled around without seeing anyone but Max, and went towards the staircase.

She collected her passport from his room. He had left it on the dressing-table. She was obviously expected to pick it up, although neither of them had thought she would be needing it so soon. Then she came back to her own room where Jenny was waiting in the doorway, and Anni's eyebrows arched in cool query as she strode past Jenny, who followed her in.

She had the smaller case open on the bed, and she was rooting through a drawer when Jenny said, 'He is a liar, isn't he?'

'One of the best,' said Anni, 'but what makes you think so?'

'What you said last night about us being stupid, I guess.' Jenny gave a little half-laugh. 'Well, I'd have to be, wouldn't I, to think you'd prefer Pete to Max? And even if you did blame Max about your brother, you didn't go on feeling so bad about that when you got to know him.'

'Pete is lying all the way,' said Anni.

It was good to be telling somebody who nodded and declared sagely, 'The jerk's shifting the blame to you. Maybe he's jealous, wants to put Max off you.'

'More likely he's saving his own skin,' said Anni. 'I don't know what he thinks Max might do to him but he'd rather it happened to somebody else. Does Max hit women?'

'Don't be ridiculous.'

'Max believes him.' That was what was crushing her, the weight there was no lifting. 'Half believes him, anyway.' Half-trust was no trust at all. 'And Jimmy?'

She waited for Jenny's verdict and Jenny said ruefully, 'He's stubborn as a mule. He's stuck with the idea that you came here to do Max down.'

For Jimmy Stapleton, Anni was no longer 'Roger's little sister', she was 'that crazy little cheat'. But Anni could manage a wry smile for that, which probably applied to Henry and Philippe too, because it was only Max's opinion that mattered. She said, 'And there is nothing I can do about it, so I am getting out. I really enjoyed socking Pete, but hitting isn't going to prove anything, and right now that's all I feel like doing.'

She dropped things into her case, smoothing down and tucking in, finding a bag of boiled sweets and pushing that down a corner. When Jenny asked, 'Where are you going?' the answer came pat.

'Idessa. This will see me through a day or two, then I'll send or come back for the rest. Max has got his papers so he doesn't have all that much to beef about, does he? By then he might have calmed down, and so might I.'

'Max is always calm,' said Jenny.

'That's nice for him,' Anni drawled. 'I used to think I was. But unless I get right away from him I am going to have a very spectacular nervous breakdown and do some very serious damage.'

'What do I tell him?'

'Stall him for a while, please. I don't think he'd bother to stop me this time, but I want to get away quietly. I'll take the back stairs and the back gate out of the gardens and catch a bus or a taxi if I can't hitch.' The way she had planned it last night.

'What do I say when he does find out you've gone?' Jenny's expression was apprehensive and Anni smiled without any humour at all.

'What makes you think he'll care? Oh, tell him I've gone to earth.'

She crept away from the house seeing no one, and if they saw her they let her go. She came out through the back gate where there was no clear track up the mountainside, and started to climb, wondering why she had lumbered herself with the little case. It would have been bad enough going downhill, climbing up it was soon going to feel as if she were carrying a load of bricks.

While she was talking to Jenny she had meant to go to Idessa, but as soon as she stepped through the gate she knew she was making for the cave. It was good to be certain of something in all this confusion. She couldn't prove Pete was lying, she couldn't make Max trust her, but all she had to concentrate on right now was remembering the way again.

She went slowly in the blazing heat, resting often, keeping under shade and cover although nobody was going to be scanning the mountainside for her. It could be hours before they missed her if Jenny made it plain enough that she wanted to be left alone. The bedroom door was locked and nobody would be pleading with her, 'Come out, Anni, please come out.'

If Jenny finally did tell them that she had gone to Idessa nobody would bother looking for her.

Max wouldn't. Anything Max had to say would
wait until she turned up again for the rest of her
luggage, and getting away from him had been the
sensible thing to do because right now she had
nothing to say to him that wouldn't have ended
in a screaming match, with her doing all the
screaming.

Pete Hartley was beneath contempt; it was Max
she was blaming. He was the one who was supposed to be so almighty smart, knowing the truth
when he heard it, but he had just accepted Pete's
accusations. 'Where's your proof that he's lying?'
he had asked her, not asking Pete to prove anything. He was so prejudiced it was mind-blowing,
and she hoped she never had to see him again.
She would rather lose the rest of her luggage if
she couldn't get it out of the villa without meeting
Max Torba.

She staggered on, fuelled by fury, until she
reached the ledge of the cave and the stunted tree
and pulled aside the curtain of brush and creepers.
Inside the cave she dropped her case and made
for the little spring. The water was delicious,
soothing the rasping pain of her parched throat,
and she closed her eyes, letting the spring play on
her face.

Then for a while she sat there, cooler now and
calmer, with time to begin wondering just what
she thought she was doing. Why hadn't she gone
to Idessa? What could she do up here, except sit
around and wait?

She couldn't be waiting for Max. He didn't
know where she was, and if he did know he

wouldn't follow her. She'd have to spend the night here, but tomorrow morning she would go back and collect her stuff, and if she met him she would say, 'I hope you never find the jewels of Helen or anything else you really want. I hope you spend the rest of your life searching and never finding.'

But she could never wish that on anybody. Nothing worse than that could happen to anyone, and the shadows seemed to close in on her and her blood ran cold as if she had just had a nightmare vision of her own future.

After that she scrambled to her feet and began moving around. She opened her case and went through it, feeling that someone else might have packed, she had been so disorientated when she was cramming in the contents. There were clothes, and a paperback, and she unwrapped a boiled sweet and slipped that into her mouth.

She might be glad of them by morning. They were all the nourishment she was likely to get, and she wondered what night would be like up here, and hoped the moon would come out when it was dark.

Now this had been crazy. This was all the proof anyone would need that she had finally flipped, but she had to get through the hours ahead, and she took her book to the mouth of the cave and sat on a flattish piece of rock where the green light was bright enough to read by.

The book was a thriller she had bought at the airport before she flew out because the first page had seemed promising. On the plane she had put it aside fairly soon, but now she read doggedly on although the characters never came to life, and she reached the last chapter still not caring 'whodunit' or why.

She had gone outside time and again, walking the ledge, looking out and knowing that if she did see anyone climbing this high they would be strangers. Hour after hour went by, and of course she was not disappointed because she was not expecting anything.

When she did see him there was no doubt at all. He was near enough to be unmistakable, and her happiness was so overwhelming that she nearly jumped off the ledge and went tumbling down towards him.

She actually hung on to the tree to keep herself back because it probably had nothing to do with her, his coming here. He'd said he came up to the cave to be alone. It didn't mean he was walking back into her life.

He saw her and raised a hand, but that still didn't mean he had expected to find her, and she stood waiting, arms folded. He had a small haversack on his shoulders and she thought, He was getting away from it all, he wasn't coming for me. 'Hi,' she said, as he reached the ledge. 'The running water's still running.'

'Thank heaven for that,' he said.

She followed him to the spring, and as he drank she asked, 'What's in the bag?'

'Food,' he said. 'You can't go on missing meals.'

'How did you know I was here?'

'I didn't when Jenny said you'd gone to Idessa.

I've been there all day, looking for you. I'm getting a reputation for being careless with my house guests. Yesterday I'm putting out the "wanted" posters for him, and today it's you. I'd got the whole team out looking for you. Then I got Jenny to repeat exactly what you'd said and when she said "gone to earth" it had to be here.' She had left that clue, just as a driving force had brought her here to wait for him, and now he was asking her in the same casual tones, 'Did you have any trouble finding it?'

'No.' This was the third time, she was getting used to the way by now. 'Did Pete go back on what he said about me?' That was the only reason she could think of why Max wanted to be with her again. When he said no she gasped, 'Then where's your proof?'

'Sorry about that,' he said. 'I don't need proof.'

'Why not? You've changed your mind.'

'About a lot of things.'

She sat with her feet tucked beneath her, because her knees were giving way and she needed all her attention for what he was saying. 'Such as?' she asked.

He considered briefly. She watched him marshalling his thoughts, getting some order into them. Then he said, 'I suppose I was half in love with you when Hartley was waiting for you on the launch. When you went down below I was suffering, imagining what was going on between you in the cabin. I couldn't leave the launch until you came up on deck again. When I met him on his way to your room that night I nearly knocked him down. I have never met a man I disliked more, and that was because I'd never come across a woman I wanted more.'

Her heart was beating in her throat so that she couldn't speak and he was not waiting for her to speak. He said, 'When it seemed you'd gone with him and the papers I couldn't believe it. There had to be an explanation. And then Jimmy gave me one and that was my world gone mad. You'd hated me while I'd been falling harder for you every day.

'And as if that wasn't enough, I was still crucified at the thought of you with another man. While I was questioning you I was less concerned about the papers than how involved you were with Pete Hartley. It was jealousy that was screwing me up.' His face was ravaged with a pain that could have broken a lesser man.

'When he started this morning about being mad for you, ready to do anything for you, he had me there, I could understand that. But after they cleared off I was euphoric, and it wasn't getting the papers back. It was because whatever there had been between you and Hartley was over.'

She put out a hand and touched his face and said, 'There never was anything.' He put out his arms and drew her against him and they were clinging together as if they were safe and sheltered in the eye of a storm. 'And I didn't tell him about the papers,' she said.

Pete could have gone into the study during the party, or in the dead of night when he ended up in her room, and Max said, 'I know that. After this I'll take your word against the world. I've behaved like a bastard, but knowing you'd hated me was ripping my guts out. I never knew you blamed me for Roger's death. I didn't realise at the time how deeply you felt.'

She had often hidden her feelings behind the mask of her face and he was a master of self-control. She said, 'Jenny said you were always calm.'

'How would Jenny know how I feel?' he demanded roughly. 'How would anyone know but you?' He cupped her face in his hands and she looked into his eyes and thought, *yes*, I read you and you read me. We could talk without words across a crowded room.

She said huskily, 'I didn't hate *you*, I didn't know *you*. And I was a little crazy at the time, not just because of losing Rog, but something my father had just said. He'd always blamed me because my mother died, and just before you came, not more than five minutes before, he said, "Why are you always the one left alive? Why couldn't it be you?" Those were almost the last words he ever did say to me.'

Now he was cradling her, rocking her, and she could feel a terrible anger burning in him, seaming the muscles of his jaw. 'Damn his soul,' he said, and he put fingertips over her parted lips as if he was reassuring himself that she was warm and breathing, and said huskily, 'Thank heaven it was not you.'

She thanked heaven too; life had never been so precious. But even now something might spoil everything, and she heard herself chattering, 'I brought a case. How about that? I came up here with an overnight bag.'

'That's organisation.'

He was smiling again and she said, 'Not really.' Her fingers were still laced with his and he was going to make love to her and she would try to be everything he wanted her to be. But she could be a disappointment and she was still putting off the moment of naked truth. 'I didn't know I was coming up here until I was out of the gardens.'

She smiled and shrugged, making a little performance of it. 'Well, I suppose the idea was at the back of my mind, that "gone to earth" bit, but I had intended going to Idessa. So I took a bag with me. Then, somehow, I found myself climbing up loaded with it.'

She scrambled to her feet and he let go of her hand and she brought the small case over. 'There's a bag of sweets,' she said. 'What did you bring? We can have a feast.'

From her case she took out a white satin dressing-gown and draped it over her shoulders. 'Very fetching,' he said.

She knew she was fetching, but he must have had hordes of girls for her to compete with. She smoothed the long skirt over her hips, looking down and muttering, 'How many lovers have you had?'

'I'm one of the world's workers, I don't have too much time for chasing women.'

He didn't need to chase them, but she narrowed the field. 'How many have you brought up here?'

'No one has come here with me.'

'But you said——'

'That there never was anyone, anywhere, like you.'

It sounded wonderful, but she reflected wryly that he could be nearly right. There must be very few sexy-looking virgins of her age. She straightened up, holding the robe to her throat, and the skirt swayed as she moved and he said, 'Are you dancing?'

She thought dizzily that she could do worse. She might be a lousy lover, but she could be a sexy dancer. She asked, 'Do you want me to dance?'

'No, thanks,' he said promptly.

He stood up and the robe slid off her shoulders, and she felt as if the shirt she wore had slipped off too. Her skin was warming, glowing.

'When you danced,' he said, 'you could have burned down Troy. Schliemann was not the bloody fool I'd always thought him for decking his wife in the jewels of Helen. That night I wanted to put them on my wife. I wanted her to follow the trail with me. I wanted her with me, always, wherever I went. Most of all, I wanted to make love to her.'

He had to mean Anni and she whispered, 'Why didn't you?'

'All that week I was taking it slowly. I wanted you hooked forever so that it had to be good for you, the right time, the right place. In the middle of the arena might have been the time, but it hardly seemed the ideal locale. Mind you, if you'd given me any encouragement a full house wouldn't have stopped me.'

His dark eyes glinted wickedly and she gurgled, 'We could have had our own little orgy.'

'A splendid idea.' He drew her down, the robe beneath her, and as he began to undo the buttons of her shirt she began to prattle nervously.

'It isn't that I don't love you because I do, terribly, but please don't feel let down because I've had no practice at all in this sort of thing so I don't think I'll be up to orgy standard.'

When she said she loved him she felt his hand tremble, and his fingers lay light and still on her breast. Now he kissed her, just as lightly. 'Then I have a dance to teach you,' he said, and in his eyes she saw such a blaze of longing that it dazzled her. 'You are so beautiful.' She nodded because she believed him. 'I want to love you,' he said and she nodded again.

She lay still while he undressed her gently, but when she felt his lips on hers the depth of his kiss seemed to reach her heart so that for a moment she thought she would faint. An intoxicating warmth was spreading through her, drowning her in delight. At first she lay breathing shallowly, enjoying her body for the first time as he caressed her with a firm and sensual touch, stroking, fondling, entering, bringing every part of her to fevered life, until she found herself reaching for him, knowing instinctively what to do to make him groan with pleasure.

This was her element, as natural as dancing, but with a piercing and erotic sweetness as everything blurred through a little pain to an explosion of joy that whirled her on a journey of raptures beyond her wildest imagining. She had come into her kingdom, and afterwards she could not bear to let him go.

He held her against him for a while, and when she opened her eyes she knew that this was how she wanted every waking to be for the rest of her life. They smiled at each other and then she asked, 'Was I all right?'

'Not all right,' he said, and she gasped. He said, 'If we never track down the jewels of Helen, I've still found the most blazingly brilliant jewel in the world. You're the treasure. You are sensational. Helen can have had nothing on you. I shall love and lust for you longer than I live.'

She looped bare arms around his neck, her fingers in his hair. 'It was lovely.' And she pulled his face to hers, making it a teasing question. 'And that was only the first lesson—what will you be teaching me next?'

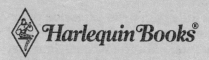
Harlequin Books®

GREAT NEWS...
HARLEQUIN UNVEILS NEW SHIPPING PLANS

For the convenience of customers, Harlequin has announced that Harlequin romances will now be available in stores at these convenient times each month*:

Harlequin Presents, American Romance, Historical, Intrigue:

> May titles: April 10
> June titles: May 8
> July titles: June 5
> August titles: July 10

Harlequin Romance, Superromance, Temptation, Regency Romance:

> May titles: April 24
> June titles: May 22
> July titles: June 19
> August titles: July 24

We hope this new schedule is convenient for you.

With only two trips each month to your local bookseller, you'll never miss any of your favorite authors!

*Please note: There may be slight variations in on-sale dates in your area due to differences in shipping and handling.

*Applicable to U.S. only.

HDATES-RR

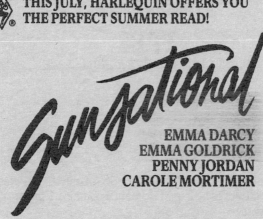

**Don't miss one exciting moment of your next vacation
with Harlequin's**

FREE
FIRST CLASS TRAVEL ALARM CLOCK

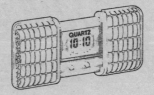

Actual Size
3 ¼" x 1 ¼" h

Just mail us 2 FIRST CLASS proofs-of-purchase—each
FIRST CLASS Harlequin Romance contains 1 proof-of-
purchase!

All you have to do is fill out the following order form,
enclose your 2 proofs-of-purchase and mail to the address listed below.

ORDER FORM

Name

Address   Apt.

City   State/Prov.   Zip/Postal Code

Daytime Phone Number _____
                    (Area Code)
